JESSI'S BIG BREAK

**Other books by
Ann M. Martin**

Leo the Magnificat
Rachel Parker, Kindergarten Show-off
Eleven Kids, One Summer
Ma and Pa Dracula
Yours Turly, Shirley
Ten Kids, No Pets
Slam Book
Just a Summer Romance
Missing Since Monday
With You and Without You
Me and Katie (the Pest)
Stage Fright
Inside Out
Bummer Summer

THE KIDS IN MS. COLMAN'S CLASS series
BABY-SITTERS LITTLE SISTER series
THE BABY-SITTERS CLUB mysteries
THE BABY-SITTERS CLUB series
CALIFORNIA DIARIES series

JESSI'S BIG BREAK

Ann M. Martin

AN
APPLE
PAPERBACK

SCHOLASTIC INC.
New York Toronto London Auckland Sydney

Cover art by Hodges Soileau

No part of this publication may be reproduced in whole or in part, or stored in a retrieval system, or transmitted in any form or by any means, electronic, mechanical, photocopying, recording, or otherwise, without written permission of the publisher. For information regarding permission, write to Scholastic Inc., Attention: Permissions Department, 555 Broadway, New York, NY 10012.

ISBN 0-590-05993-9

12 11 10 9 8 7 6 5 4 3 2 1   8 9/9 0 1/0 2/0

Printed in the U.S.A.   40

First Scholastic printing, January 1998

*The author gratefully acknowledges
Peter Lerangis
for his help in
preparing this manuscript.*

CHAPTER 1

"I'm ho-ome!"

I let the front door close behind me and shook the snow off my coat.

"Hiiii!" shouted my little sister, Becca, from inside.

My aunt Cecelia was bustling around in the kitchen. I knew just what she'd say. I always know.

Today was a *wipe your shoes* day.

"Wipe your shoes, Jessica!" called Aunt Cecelia's voice.

"Yes, Aunt Cecelia," I replied.

And close both doors, I thought. *We're not working for the gas and electric company.*

"And close both doors! We're not working for Stoneybrook Gas and Electric!"

"Yes, Aunt Cecelia."

And hang up your coat.

"And check the mail, dear! There's something for you."

Oh, well. Two out of three wasn't bad.

I moved toward the closet. The mail was piled on the phone stand. I glanced at the letter on top. It was addressed to me. Then I looked at the return address.

Three words. In sleek blue letters that seemed to leap off the paper.

Dance New York.

The Dance New York. World-famous ballet company and school.

The blood rushed from my head. I nearly dropped my coat.

I thought I was going to faint.

It had been almost a month since I'd auditioned for Dance New York's special winter session. I figured they'd forgotten about me. Which made sense, considering how many people had shown up to audition. Hundreds.

Seeing that letter brought it all back. The noisy, jammed theater. The long wait. The feeling that I didn't belong there.

I felt so inferior to some of those dancers. I'm eleven, which meant I had to audition in the eleven-to-thirteen-year-old category. I am advanced for my age, but still. The older kids have much cleaner lines and more solid technique. Totally unfair, if you ask me.

The night of the audition I cried myself to sleep. Daddy and Mama both had to comfort me. They both told me not to give up hope.

As you can see, I take dance very seriously. I practice *tour jetés* on the way to school. I *plié* in the cafeteria line. I do stretching exercises whenever I'm standing still. I take ballet lessons in Stamford, Connecticut. (That's the city closest to the town where I live, Stoney-brook.) But I've been a dance fanatic since before birth. Mama felt me high-kicking when she was pregnant. As a baby I would do *arabesques* in my playpen.

(Time-out. For you nondancers, those French words are not names of pastries. They describe ballet movements. Basically, an *arabesque* is a forward bend with one leg extended backward. A *tour jeté* is a series of leaps, and a *plié* is a knee bend.)

I still shiver when I think about the time I saw a Dance New York performance. It was in New York City several months ago. My parents took me to see it. The founder and main chore-ographer, David Brailsford, is a genius. A legend. His dances combine jazz, African rhythms, and classical ballet.

Really, I should have been happy just for the opportunity to audition for Dance New York.

At least that was what I had told myself.

Now, seeing the mail, I felt my stomach contracting. I was afraid to touch the envelope. Afraid of what might be inside. *We regret to inform you, Ms. Ramsey . . .*

"What are you doing, Jessica? Waiting for it to grow?"

Aunt Cecelia was standing in the front hallway now, hands on her hips. Becca was scooting around her.

"Open it!" Becca demanded.

I lifted the envelope. It was thick.

I ripped it open, pulled out a wad of official-looking papers, and began to read.

" 'Dear Ms. Ramsey . . .' " My voice was thin and squeaky. " 'We are pleased to inform you of your acceptance into the Dance New York A-Level winter session, for girls and boys ages eleven to thirteen . . .' "

I stopped there. I could not go on. The next thing that came out of my mouth was a huge, ear-splitting scream. I couldn't help it.

I thought for sure Aunt Cecelia would scold me. Instead, she chuckled and shook her head. "Mercy, with that voice you may as well add opera lessons."

I threw my arms around Aunt Cecelia and almost knocked her over. *"I did it! I did it! I'm going to New York!"*

Becca's face was suddenly clouding over. "Wait. You have to leave us?"

"Well, yeah," I replied. "But just for awhile."

I sat on the sofa and read the letter aloud, beginning to end. All the details. Three and a half

4

weeks of intensive study. "On-site tutors" provided "from a prestigious local teachers' college." Classes held in "the heart of SoHo, New York's most vital arts district."

At that point Aunt Cecelia's eyebrows rose way up. "And where, pray tell, are you supposed to sleep at night?"

"It doesn't say. Maybe I can commute."

"Well, we'll put that question to your father and mother," Aunt Cecelia said.

"But I *have* to go!" I protested. "This is a once-in-a-lifetime opportunity."

"I understand. Oh, I wish I had a quarter for all the once-in-a-lifetime opportunities I let pass by. I'd be a wealthy woman. You know, I wanted to be an actress. When I played Harriet Tubman in my junior high school . . ."

There wasn't a dry eye in the house.

I knew the whole story by heart. I'd heard it a thousand times.

"This is boring, Aunt Cecelia," said Becca.

"I'll never forget my teacher's words," Aunt Cecelia droned on. " 'Cecelia Ramsey, someday I will see your name in lights.' "

"So why *didn't* you become an actress?" I asked.

"Life," Aunt Cecelia replied. "It has a way of beating you down. You have to fight it, Jessi. You'll see."

I watched her trudge away toward the kitchen. In her drab housedress and clunky shoes.

My aunt. She can find the gray lining in every silver cloud.

Now, I love Aunt Cecelia. She's always there when Becca and I come home from school. She takes care of us when we're sick. She adores Squirt, my baby brother.

But she can be a real pain.

Why does she live with us? Well, she moved in after the death of her husband, my uncle Steven. At the same time, Mom was going back to work (she'd taken a leave of absence when Squirt was born). Aunt Cecelia needed company, we needed help around the house — so Daddy invited her to live with us. (She's his older sister.)

Daddy jokes that the *real* reason Aunt Cecelia's here is because no one else will have her.

You know what? I don't think that's a joke. At least, not entirely. Aunt Cecelia *does* have two other brothers, my uncles Arthur and Charles. They didn't ask her to move in, and their houses are as big as ours.

I don't blame them. Whenever I hear Aunt Cecelia talk to them on the phone, she's always scolding.

She's even worse with her own son, my cousin Michael. She hardly talks to him. I could never figure out why. He's grown-up and married to a nice woman named Marian, and they recently moved to a big apartment in . . .

Brooklyn!

"Aunt Cecelia?" I blurted out. "Is Brooklyn close to New York City?"

"Brooklyn is *part* of New York City," Aunt Cecelia replied, turning from the kitchen doorway. "Do you mean, how far is Brooklyn from *Manhattan*? Because if you do, it is quite accessible by subway."

I practically leaped off the sofa. "Then I can live with Michael and Marian!"

Aunt Cecelia's lips pursed. She looked away. "Jessica, you are counting your chickens before they are hatched. First let's see if your father and mother will approve of this program. I personally hope they do, but if I were you, I would not get my hopes up. Now, do your homework —"

"EEEEEEEE!"

Squirt was screaming from his crib. Nap time was over.

"I'll get him!" Becca and I shouted at the same time.

We ran to his room. His face broke into a big grin when he saw us. "Dess-see! Bet-ta!"

I picked him up and started waltzing him around the room, making up a silly tune. "Dance with meeeeee . . . laaaa-la-leeeee."

"Jessi's going to be leaving us, Squirt," Becca said.

I sang louder. Squirt was giggling like crazy.

"She's going away for a month!" Becca pressed on. "Dess-see go bye-bye."

"Becca, will you stop?" I said.

"Dess-see? Bye-bye?" Squirt's smile vanished. "No!"

I glared at my sister. "Thanks a lot."

"Well, it's true," Becca said, storming out.

I did not expect that reaction from Becca. I thought she'd be excited for me.

But she was angry.

An angry sister. An aunt who was a pill.

Wasn't anybody thinking about *me*? I'd just received the greatest news of my life. I was thrilled. I should have been dancing with joy.

So why were they making me feel as if I'd done something wrong?

I couldn't wait to see the looks on my parents' faces when I told them the news in person. I would be able to tell them at the same time too. Today they were going to be driving home from work together.

I was putting on a Dance New York T-shirt in my bedroom when the car pulled into the driveway. As I ran downstairs, I could hear Becca opening the front door and shouting, "Guess what? Jessi's running away from home!"

I ran past her and out the door. I wasn't wearing a coat, but I didn't care. *"I made Dance New York!"*

Daddy lifted me off the ground and swung me around. "I am so-o-o-o proud of you!"

Mama wrapped her arms around both of us. "I knew you'd do it, sweetheart."

"She can't go!" Becca called out. "She's going to live on the sidewalk and eat rats."

Squirt darted out the front door, screaming, "Day-ee! Ma-ma!" before Aunt Cecelia pulled him back.

"I can go, can't I?" I asked.

Mama gave Daddy a Look.

Daddy sighed heavily. "Okay, troops, family meeting time!"

Uh-oh.

I knew what that meant. *You're too young.*

I was not going to give in. I was going to stand my ground. My parents are great, but they've always treated me as if I were a baby. That's the worst thing about being the oldest child. Becca gets away with murder compared to me.

Aunt Cecelia, Becca, Squirt, and I settled in the living room. Mama and Daddy both ducked inside the kitchen to fetch snacks. I could hear them muttering under their breath. The way they do whenever they argue.

I braced myself for the battle.

When they returned to the living room, the words poured out of my mouth. "I have thought about this for a long time. I know I'm only eleven. I know I'll have to leave school for almost a month and adjust to tutors. I know my workload will be heavy. But I'm not a baby. I can do it."

"Jessica," Mama said. "You'll be alone in a strange city —"

"It's not strange," I protested. "I've been there lots of times. And I won't be alone either. I'll be in class all day and with Michael and Marian at night —"

"Michael and Marian?" Daddy asked. "Have you called them?"

"Well, no, not yet," I replied. "But I *could* stay with them."

"They're a young couple," Aunt Cecelia said. "They have their busy-busy lives, never home, working into the night on goodness knows what. Michael never even has enough time to talk to his own mother. How could they possibly handle you?"

"Call and ask!" I pleaded.

"I could try, but I always get their answering machine," Aunt Cecelia said. "Answering machines make me very uncomfortable."

"Stay with us," said Becca.

"Dess-see," said Squirt.

I looked hopefully at my mom and dad.

Mama took my hand. "Look, your father and I have been discussing this possibility since your audition. It's a major thing for an eleven-year-old to do — living in the big city, not knowing anyone . . ."

My stomach was sinking.

"But we knew that if we said no," Daddy continued, "we would regret it the rest of our lives."

"So . . . I can go?"

Daddy stood up and kissed me on the forehead. "Let me call Michael's answering machine right now. Maybe if he hears that it's not his meddling mom on the phone, he'll pick up."

"Well, I *never*," Aunt Cecelia huffed.

"Lucky!" Becca said, stomping out of the room.

"Dutty!" Squirt echoed.

Me? I don't remember what I said. I was floating somewhere near the ceiling.

I have never been so happy in all my life.

CHAPTER 2

"Do you even know Michael?" asked Stacey McGill.

"Not really," I said. "He went away to college when I was little. All I remember is that Aunt Cecelia used to yell at him a lot."

"She yells at everybody," Mallory Pike remarked.

"My dad says that's why Michael doesn't keep in touch," I said. "I mean, Aunt Cecelia should be *proud* of Michael. He works as a financial something, and his wife sells advertising for a magazine. They have a big apartment in a nice neighborhood, and Aunt Cecelia keeps saying he's thrown his life away!"

"What did she expect him to do?" asked Claudia Kishi.

"Become the first African-American President of the United States, I guess," I replied. "I don't know."

"This meeting will come to order!" shouted Kristy Thomas.

It was exactly five-thirty on a Friday, eight days after my acceptance to Dance New York. In two days I was scheduled to leave for New York City.

This was my last official Baby-sitters Club meeting for almost a month.

I felt a little funny. The BSC is a huge part of my life. For starters, we meet three times a week (Mondays, Wednesdays, and Fridays) from five-thirty until six. But more than that, we're as close as sisters. Sometimes I feel as if we'll be doing this for the rest of our lives.

What exactly do we do? Well, talk, for one thing. Laugh (a lot). And eat junk food (a *lot*). Oh. And book baby-sitting jobs.

Actually, that's the whole point of the BSC. Seven qualified, experienced baby-sitters together in one room, ready to answer phone calls from local parents who need our services.

We have lots of repeat clients. They've memorized our meeting hours. (More or less. Claudia still has to answer a stray call or two between meetings.) Claudia's bedroom is our official headquarters because she's the only member with her own private phone line.

For a roomful of gabbing girls, we're super-organized. We have officers, we pay dues, and

13

we write about every single sitting job in an official BSC notebook. Everybody reads the entries once a week. That's how we keep each other up-to-date about our clients — house rules, rate changes, our charges' new fears and allergies, who's had chicken pox and strep throat, and so on.

The reason we're so efficient is two words: Kristy Thomas. She's our president and founder. She's also the Idea Genius of the Free World.

Kristy invented the Baby-sitters Club one day when her mom couldn't find a sitter for Kristy's little brother, David Michael. Kristy herself had some other commitment, and so did her two older brothers, Charlie and Sam. (Mr. Thomas had long ago abandoned the family, so he was out of the picture.) As Kristy watched her poor mom make call after call, *blink*! On went the light. Why not create some kind of central baby-sitting agency?

A couple of phone calls to friends, and the BSC was born. Claudia, Stacey, Kristy, and Mary Anne Spier were the original members. But the club became popular very fast. Mallory and I joined, and so did Dawn Schafer. Since then, Dawn has moved and Abby Stevenson has taken her place. But I'm getting ahead of myself.

As president, Kristy is our queen bee. Basically she (1) bosses everyone around, (2) thinks up big ideas, and (3) bosses everyone around again. For someone who's only five feet tall, she can be overpowering. It's a good thing she's so lovable.

One of Kristy's specialties is advertising. She hands a BSC flyer to every adult she meets. She plans a BSC booth at every local fair or block party. Her other specialty? Kids. She knows just what they need, and they adore her. Kristy invented Kid-Kits, which are boxes filled with old toys, games, books, and knickknacks we sometimes take with us on our jobs. (To kids, they're like little treasure chests.) When some of our younger charges showed an interest in softball, no problem. Kristy happens to be a sports nut, so she organized a team for them, called Kristy's Krushers.

Kristy thrives on noise and activity. Her house is total pandemonium. Actually, *house* isn't the word for it. *Mansion* is more like it.

No, Kristy did not win the lottery. Her mom got remarried, to a guy who is very rich. His name is Watson Brewer. His two children from his previous marriage live at the mansion during alternate months. Plus he and Kristy's mom adopted a little girl from Vietnam. Her name is Emily Michelle. Then Kristy's grandmother moved in to help take care of Emily.

Add a few pets, and you have an idea of what it's like at the Thomas/Brewer residence.

Actually, the prize for Most Crowded House in the BSC has to go to Mallory. She has seven younger brothers and sisters, all loud. I don't know how anyone can think in that house.

Mal is my best friend in the world. We're like sisters. We're also the only "junior officers" of the BSC. That's because all the *other* members are eighth-graders, two years older than us. Which shouldn't make much of a difference. But it does. You see, Mr. and Mrs. Pike treat Mal like a baby too. Like my parents, they won't allow their oldest daughter to baby-sit at night, unless it's for her own siblings. (Grrr.)

If you read one of Mallory's stories, you'd know how mature she really is. Mature and talented. Her dream is to be a children's book writer and illustrator someday. I personally hope she becomes the next Marguerite Henry or Bonnie Bryant. (Mal and I both adore horse stories.)

I could go on and on with the things Mallory and I have in common. One of the few things we *don't* have in common is our looks. Mal's skin is pale white and freckly. Her hair is reddish-brown and super-thick and she wears glasses. (I don't.) And you would never mistake her for a dancer. I keep telling her to straighten her posture, but she never listens.

At the BSC meeting that Friday, she was gently pushing my ankles upward, helping me do leg lifts. Mary Anne and Stacey were lifting their feet because Claudia needed to look under her bed for something. Shannon Kilbourne, who had been standing at the foot of the bed, was scrunched up against the wall. Abby was dancing to a tune coming through the radio. Kristy was sitting in her director's chair, tapping a pencil on Claudia's desk.

"Any new business?" Kristy called out.

"Yes," Claudia said, yanking out a huge bag of candy. "Snickers! To celebrate Jessi's last meeting before she goes to New York. They were half price all week. I got the last nine bags."

Abby looked around the room curiously. "*Nine* bags?"

"Well, we don't have to eat them all now," Claudia explained.

"This is not *business*," Kristy snapped. "I asked for new business!"

Rrrrring! went the phone.

Claudia snatched up the receiver. "Baby-sitters Club, Incorporated. Your kids are our business."

Kristy cringed. The rest of us cracked up.

"No, Mrs. Kuhn, just joking," Claudia said. "Next Thursday night? Okay, I'll get right back to you."

17

As she hung up, Mary Anne began checking the BSC record book.

That's how we handle our job requests. First stop is always Mary Anne, our club secretary. Inside the record book she keeps a master calendar. She marks all our jobs and conflicts in it — medical appointments, after-school activities, family trips, and so on. She knows at a glance which of us is available. Not only that, she distributes the jobs evenly among us. *Plus* she keeps an updated client list in the back of the book. It includes addresses, phone numbers, rates charged, and important information about our charges (such as their birthdays and favorite foods).

If Kristy is the queen bee of the group, Mary Anne is the number one worker bee. She makes sure everything runs smoothly. Actually, Kristy and Mary Anne have been best friends practically since birth. They even look a little alike — same height, same dark brown eyes and hair. But you would never mix them up in a million years. Mary Anne is quiet, for one thing, and she hates sports. She's also a good listener and cries at the slightest thing. Her boyfriend, Logan Bruno, takes along a jumbo box of tissues when they go to sad movies together.

Mary Anne's life would make a sad movie. Her mom died when Mary Anne was a baby. Her dad, Richard, fell apart. He had to let Mary

Anne's grandparents raise her while he recovered. Then, when he said he was ready to take her back, they refused to give her up. They didn't believe he could raise her alone. He finally convinced them, but he thought he had to become the world's strictest parent, to prove he could do the job. He raised Mary Anne with tons of rules — early curfews, strict homework hours, phone call limits, no pants to school, conservative hairstyles.

Eventually he loosened up. Even better, he got married again — to his old high school sweetheart, who happened to move back to Stoneybrook after divorcing her husband in California.

Even better than that, his old high school sweetheart happened to be the mother of Dawn Schafer, a BSC member! Now, *that's* a romantic story. Around the time Dawn joined the BSC, she and Mary Anne found out about the long-ago Lost Love. They played matchmaker, and the rest is history. Mary Anne gained a sister, a brother (Jeff Schafer, who's ten), and a mom. She also got to move into the Schafers' cool two-hundred-year-old farmhouse.

I wish I could say it all had a happy ending. But first Jeff decided to return to Mr. Schafer in California. Then Dawn did. That really broke up Mary Anne (the rest of us were also pretty devastated). Dawn does manage to visit a lot, though. And Mary Anne loves having a step-mom. Sharon (Mrs. Schafer Spier) is fun-loving and absentminded, just the opposite of Richard. Mary Anne can look and dress the way she wants to. (Her style is a conservative, preppy look, which Claudia calls "L.L. J. Crew Bauer.")

Claudia, by the way, is our vice-president. But a better title might be Snack Czar. She is devoted to junk food. Her parents, unfortunately, don't allow it in the house. So Claudia hides it wherever she can.

Which is not hard. Her room has lots of nooks. It's a total mess. For each meeting, she has to push aside sketchbooks, canvases, sculptures, and all kinds of artworks-in-progress. You see, art is Claudia's other love. Even her outfits are like collages. She puts them together from stuff she finds in thrift shops and at yard sales. That day, for example, she was wearing a leopard-skin jumpsuit with a black silk shirt tied at the waist with leather strips; black, steel-tipped combat boots; and rhinestone-studded cat's-eye glasses perched on her head. (Claudia doesn't actually wear glasses.) If I wore that outfit, people would laugh. But on Claudia, it looks *right*.

If you met Claudia's family, you wouldn't believe they are related to her. Mr. Kishi's a banker and Mrs. Kishi's a librarian. Claudia's sister, Janine the Genius, is in eleventh grade but she takes college courses. They're all super-conservative and dedicated to high achievement. Claudia, on the other hand, has always had trouble with academics. For awhile, she even had to be sent back to seventh grade.

Claudia used to have a soul mate in the family, her grandmother, Mimi. Mimi seemed very "old country" (the Kishis are Japanese-American), but she appreciated Claudia's creativity. After Mimi died, Claudia put a photo of her on her bedroom wall. It always inspires her when she's feeling confused or lonely.

Claudia's best friend is Stacey McGill. When it comes to junk food, they're like Jack Sprat and his wife. Stacey cannot eat sweets. She has a condition called diabetes. Her body doesn't produce the proper amount of an important hormone called insulin, which is like a traffic cop for sugar. When a nondiabetic person eats something sweet, the insulin lets some of the sugar into the bloodstream, while holding back the rest until later. In a diabetic, all the sugar rushes right into the blood, which is not a good thing. Fortunately, Stacey can lead a normal life as long as she eats at regular times, monitors what she eats, and injects herself daily with artificial insulin. It sounds gross, I know, but Stacey says it's as painless as brushing your teeth.

Looking at Stacey, you'd never imagine she

has any kind of health condition. She's gorgeous. Her hair is golden blonde and her smile is about, oh, five hundred watts. If you spot a new fashion trend, chances are Stacey's discovered it already. She loves sleek, urban clothes, and black is her favorite color.

Stacey likes to say she grew up on the cutting edge of fashion (otherwise known as New York City). She lived there until seventh grade, when her dad's company transferred him to Connecticut. Stacey adjusted to the suburbs, joined the BSC, and then — *whoosh* — another transfer back to the city. We thought we'd lost her forever. But soon she was back again, this time with only her mother. Yup, divorce. Mr. and Mrs. McGill hadn't been getting along for awhile, and they finally split up. (Stacey's dad still lives in the city, so she gets to visit a lot.)

Stacey's our treasurer, mainly because she loves math. Each Monday she collects dues. At the end of the month she pays Claudia for the phone, allots some money to buy Kid-Kit stuff, and gives Kristy's brother Charlie a gas allowance for driving Kristy and Abby to meetings.

Abby lives way over in Kristy's neck of the woods. She moved to Stoneybrook from Long Island with her twin sister, Anna, and their mom. Just in time too, because Dawn had left and we were overloaded with baby-sitting jobs. We asked both girls to join, but Anna said no. She's a serious musician who dedicates her free time to practicing violin.

Abby is so different from her quiet sister. She's, well, *big*. Not physically, but personality-wise. She's outgoing and friendly and athletic, and she can find the humor in anything. Even her hair is big. It flows to her shoulders in thick, uncontrollable ringlets. Sometimes Abby calls it "the Beast."

Since Abby joined the club, Claudia has tried to keep her room dust-free. That's because Abby's allergic to dust — as well as to dogs and strawberries and a thousand other things. She has asthma too and always carries a set of inhalers with her.

Lately Abby has been reading about the connection between illness and the mind. She thinks her asthma might be affected by the sadness she feels. You see, her dad was killed in a car crash when she and Anna were nine. Whenever she talks about that (which isn't often), you can see the pain in her eyes.

Abby's spiritual side really came out at her Bat Mitzvah. That's a coming-of-age ceremony held for Jewish girls when they turn thirteen. She and Anna invited all us BSC members to theirs. Even though I didn't understand the Hebrew they recited, I found the ceremony very moving.

Abby, by the way, is the BSC's alternate officer. She takes over for any officer who's absent.

The BSC has two associate members, Logan and Shannon. They aren't required to pay dues or attend meetings, but they help us out whenever they can. Logan, as I mentioned before, is Mary Anne's boyfriend. He's friendly and outgoing, but he's way too involved in after-school sports to be a regular member. Besides, his teammates tease him about being in the BSC, and that bothers him (even though he denies it). Shannon, who lives across the street from Kristy, goes to a private school called Stoneybrook Day School. (The rest of us attend Stoneybrook Middle School.)

Shannon had made a special appearance at Friday's meeting, just to say good-bye to me. "So, are you going to come visit us on weekends?" she asked.

"Puh-leeze. Would *you*?" Claudia cut in. "She's going to be going out every night. Clubs, parties, shows. Besides, she can see that guy — Clint? What was his name?"

I was thinking, *Clubs, parties? Is Claudia crazy?* But all I said was, "Quint." I could feel myself blushing. Quint Walter was a boy I'd met in the audience of a New York City Ballet performance. He's a dancer too. He lives in Manhattan and studies at Juilliard, which is a famous school for dance, music, and drama in

New York City. We kind of liked each other. Well, more than liked. He's the only boy I've ever kissed. We wrote and called for awhile, but it was just too hard to keep up a long-distance relationship. Besides, I wasn't ready to have a steady boyfriend. We agreed to stay friends, but eventually we lost touch.

"Anyway, Shannon," I said, quickly changing the subject, "I won't be home next weekend. Dance New York has planned activities for us on Saturday and Sunday."

"What about the weekend after?" Mary Anne asked.

I shrugged. "I haven't really thought about it."

"Uh-oh, she's forgetting us already," Abby murmured.

"We'll keep a candle burning in the window," Stacey added with a dramatic sigh. "Maybe someday you'll return."

"Oh, you guys are worse than Becca. She acts like I'll never see her again."

"Will you?" Claudia asked.

The phone rang before I could respond.

Which was just as well. I was tired of these jokes.

Of course I wasn't going to stay in NYC.

I wouldn't dream of it.

CHAPTER 3

"Jessi! Mal's here!" yelled my mother from downstairs.

"Come . . . on . . . up!" I said, yanking my suitcase zipper.

I plopped down onto my bedroom floor. No way was that suitcase going to close.

Should I have packed the Saturday night before I had to leave? Of course. Did I? No-o-o-o.

Now it was Sunday. I'd spent all morning throwing things into two suitcases, a garment bag, and a backpack. No one was helping me. Mama and Daddy were busy getting ready for the drive to New York. Becca was having a tantrum. Aunt Cecelia was clattering around after Squirt.

I heard footsteps on the stairs. My door opened and Mal walked in. "Hi."

"They told me to pack light!" I said. "How do you pack light for a winter in New York

City? You need sweaters, a raincoat, a down vest, boots, *plus* the ballet stuff."

Mal knelt down and began looking through my clothes. "Well, you only need a few shirts, really. You'll be dressed in your ballet clothes most of the day and you can do laundry . . ."

One by one, Mallory removed items of clothing and put them on the bed. Then she zipped the suitcase right up.

"Will you come with me?" I asked. "I need a personal assistant."

Mal adjusted her glasses and gave a funny little half smile. "Mm-hm."

Together we brought all but one suitcase downstairs and to the front door. "I would help you," Aunt Cecelia said, walking the opposite way, "but my ankles are acting up."

I gave Mallory a Look. An *I've heard that excuse before* Look.

I thought she'd smile. But she just walked past me.

Daddy rushed into the front hall, buttoning up his coat. "I'll take that, Jessi. Can't do ballet with a strained back. Hi, Mal!"

He and Mallory headed outside. I headed for the stairs to get the other suitcase.

"Yes, you *are* going, Rebecca Ramsey!" came my mother's voice from the den. "I cannot leave you here alone!"

"I don't care!" Becca retorted.

Uh-oh.

I zoomed upstairs. Fortunately, my other suitcase was smaller, so I quickly ran it out to the car.

By that time, Mama was calling Daddy into the den to talk to Becca. Mallory and I were alone by the car.

I was so excited, I wanted to scream. Mallory was staring at the sidewalk.

"Well," I said with a shrug, "this is it, I guess."

Mallory took a deep breath. When she looked at me, her eyes were brimming with tears. "This is so ridiculous. You're only going for a few weeks, but it feels as if you're moving away forever."

"Oh, Mal, is *that* why you're so quiet?"

Mal's face turned red. I put my arms around her, and she started giggling and crying at the same time. "I am *so* embarrassed."

I heard the front door open, and I turned to see Becca stomping out in an open down coat.

"Becca, zip up that parka this minute!" Aunt Cecelia called from behind her.

"No!" Becca snapped. She didn't even look at me as she climbed into the backseat of the car.

Mama bustled out after her, holding Squirt. Daddy followed, holding the collapsible stroller. Then came Aunt Cecelia, holding nothing. I hugged Mallory again and we exchanged a flurry of good-byes and I'll-miss-yous.

Into the car I went. I helped Mama strap Squirt into his car seat and *zoom* — we were off.

"Onward to superstardom!" Daddy cried, honking his horn for no reason at all.

"Beebeeeep!" yelled Squirt.

Mama smiled and waved out the window. "Mallory looks upset."

"Why can't *she* come, and I'll stay with the Pikes?" Becca grumbled. "I don't want to go to stupid Brooklyn."

"I'm glad you're here," I said gently. "It means we can spend more time together. I'm going to miss you, you know."

Becca looked out the opposite window. "So?"

"So we can try to enjoy this time together."

"So?"

Daddy flicked on the radio. "Let's hear something sweet," he said.

"Feet," answered Squirt. He began squirming and whining, trying to kick off his sneakers.

I could tell it was not going to be an easy ride.

I do not remember going over the Throg's Neck Bridge in New York. (Which is too bad.

29

I've never seen a throg.) I don't remember the crowded buildings and congested highways. In fact, I can't recall much of the ride at all. I must have fallen fast asleep on I-95.

I was awakened by a sharp bump. I thought we'd crashed. I uncurled from my sleeping position and sat up.

We were on a street lined with thin trees. Behind them were elegant three- and four-story brownstone apartment buildings. Cars were parked bumper-to-bumper on either side. Daddy was trying to angle into a teeny parking space, going back and forth inches at a time, bumping the car behind us.

"Don't *hit* the car, John," Mama said.

"It's only a love tap," Daddy replied.

"How can people live like this?" Aunt Cecelia grumbled. "All crowded up, no privacy . . ."

Frankly, I loved the neighborhood. Especially the filigreed iron railings that ran up the stone steps of each building. And the huge, carved wood doors.

"Too many stairs," Becca remarked.

After a few more love taps, the car was finally in. We all climbed out and took my luggage from the trunk.

Michael's house was three blocks away. Three long blocks, through New York City slush. Then up a steep stoop to Michael's front door.

"With all the money he makes, he can't find a nice elevator building with a doorman?" Aunt Cecelia said.

Daddy pressed the buzzer labeled PARKER.

"Hello?" came a female voice.

"It's John Ramsey!" Daddy announced in this booming radio-announcer's voice.

EHHHHHHHHHH! went an extremely loud noise — the sound of the buzzer, which unlocked the front door. Daddy pushed the door open.

We walked into a small vestibule, carpeted with thick Persian rugs. A mirror hung on the wall, which was covered in gorgeous Laura Ashley-style wallpaper.

To our left was a thick banister of dark polished wood. Footsteps came thumping downstairs. "Welcome!" said a deep voice that sounded a lot like Daddy's.

I could not believe my cousin. I remembered him as skinny and gawky. Now he was tall and powerful-looking. He hurried to Aunt Cecelia and practically lifted her off the floor. "How's the most beautiful mama on this earth?"

"Mercy, I have only one spine, child!"

What a greeting to give your own son. But Michael just laughed, and I could see the trace of a smile on Aunt Cecelia's face.

Michael picked up Squirt and fussed over

him. Then he turned to my sister and me, grinning. "Jessica! Becky!"

"-*Ca*." Becca scowled. "No one in the whole wide world calls me Becky and I'm thirsty."

Ugh. Off to a great start.

Michael hugged each of us, then introduced Becca, Squirt, and me to Marian, who had walked down the stairs behind him. She was pretty and delicate-looking, with a nice, open smile. She congratulated me and said she adored ballet.

I liked her right away.

But a funny thing happened when she turned toward Aunt Cecelia. Her smile tightened and her eyes lost their excitement. "Hello, Mother Parker."

"Nice to see you, dear," Aunt Cecelia said flatly. "How many flights must I walk?"

"Just one, Mama," Michael replied, smiling mischievously. "Or shall I carry you?"

"Making fun of me already," Aunt Cecelia muttered, trudging up the steps. "After all I've done."

I saw Marian glance nervously at Michael. He put his arm around her reassuringly. Then he grabbed a suitcase and followed Aunt Cecelia.

"I hope everybody's hungry," Michael said over his shoulder. "We have the world's best take-out Chinese restaurant in Brooklyn just around the corner."

"Chinese food?" Becca whined. "Ew."

"Bec-*ca*," Daddy said sternly.

"Honestly, Michael, a simple homemade meal would have sufficed," Aunt Cecelia said.

"Mama, when you taste this food, you'll thank us," Michael said.

"I'm really sorry," Marian added. "See, Michael and I both had to work this morning, and —"

"My parents *never* work on Sundays," Becca said.

I was so embarrassed. I felt like melting into the carpet. My cousin and his wife were putting me up for almost a month, and everyone was giving them grief.

I wouldn't have been surprised if they changed their minds about the whole thing.

Fortunately Michael was very patient. And he was right about the Chinese food. It was excellent. Even Becca ate it. And eventually, Aunt Cecelia stopped complaining.

Afterward, we chatted about Michael's and Marian's jobs. We played with Squirt. Michael showed me my room, which had two beds and was decorated with the coolest paintings. He also gave me a set of apartment keys. Then we took a walk through the neighborhood, all the way to the waterfront. There, we had a spectacular view of the Manhattan skyline.

I could not take my eyes off it. The buildings seemed like living creatures, warm and breathing. I leaned against the wooden railing and stared.

Marian stood next to me. "Just think," she said. "Starting tomorrow, you'll be in the center of it all."

I felt my cheeks flush just thinking about it. Somewhere in the middle of all that steel and concrete, above the honking horns and rumbling trains, I, Jessi Ramsey, was going to be soaring across a dance floor with the great David Brailsford.

I clutched the railing as tightly as I could. If I hadn't, I think I would have floated over the river right then and there.

CHAPTER 4

"*B*orelaffanetrafferdeewassaclodonattapursablon!*" blared the voice over the subway speakers.

"What language was that?" I asked Michael.

"New York Subway," Michael replied. "He said, 'Broadway-Lafayette is next. Transfer for the D. Watch the closing doors and take your personal belongings.' That's our stop, by the way."

"Oh."

It was the morning of my first full day in New York City, and already I could see I had a lot to learn. Translating subway announcements was one thing. Walking fast was another. I'd nearly been knocked off my feet when I'd stopped to adjust my backpack on the subway steps.

Avoiding eye contact seemed very important too. *No one* in the subway looks at another person during rush hour. They act as if they don't notice each other. Which is totally ridiculous, because you're standing shoulder to shoulder, smelling each other's cologne and breakfast breath.

By the time we reached the Broadway-Lafayette stop, I was sweaty and exhausted.

The moment we were above ground, though, Michael came to life. "SoHo is that way," he said, pointing. "Beyond it is Little Italy and Chinatown. That way is the Public Theater, and there's the Angelika Film Center. . . ."

We walked past art galleries, boutiques, vintage-clothing stores. All of them were on the ground floors of incredibly old cast-iron buildings. Michael said the area used to be an abandoned industrial district until artists began taking it over in the seventies.

For a businessguy, Michael knew a lot about artists. He took me from window to window, describing who had done what painting, in what style.

We almost missed the entrance to the Dance New York studio. It was a grimy door between a publishing company building and a hardware store. We had to wait in a teeny lobby with yellowed tiles and dim lighting. The elevator wasn't even automatic. An old, bored-looking man yanked the door open, not even looking at us. We had to cram into a tiny metal cage.

"Ninth floor, please," Michael said cheerfully. He didn't seem fazed at all, but my good mood was fading. If the dance studio was like this, I was going to head back to Stoneybrook.

One of my favorite books ever is *The Lion, the Witch, and the Wardrobe*. I've read it about four times. When Lucy Pevensie finds the wardrobe in a musty old room and walks through it into the land of Narnia, I shiver. Well, that was exactly how I felt when the elevator door opened.

Piano music echoed loudly. So did the rhythmic thudding of feet. Behind a plate glass wall, ballet dancers leaped so high they looked as if they'd been lifted with strings. The polished wood floors below them were like mirrors.

"Youth program is down the hall to the left," said a woman standing near a watercooler.

We walked past five or six practice rooms, most with their doors open. I wanted to stop and gawk before each one. I saw dancers with legs that seemed to go on forever. Outfits that made my Danskins look babyish. Triple pirouettes without the slightest effort.

"I recognize some of these dancers!" I whispered. "They're famous."

"No kidding." Michael looked impressed.

We turned a corner and entered a room marked DANCE NEW YORK YOUTH.

I was not the first one. In fact, about a dozen kids were stretching and doing *barre* exercises.

They looked just as amazing as the dancers in the practice rooms, only smaller. Their parents were sipping coffee from paper cups and talking among themselves. In the corner, a man was playing softly on an upright piano.

"It's magic time, Jessica Ramsey," Michael said with a big grin.

"These kids are too good," I murmured. "What am I doing here?"

Michael put a reassuring arm around my shoulder. "Hey, they ain't seen nothing yet."

"I wish you could stay."

Michael pretended to look horrified. "They might make me dance. Then you'd be sorry you ever knew me." He smiled. "Besides, I have to get to work. I'll pick you up at five-thirty. Knock 'em dead."

As Michael scooted away, a young woman walked to me with a clipboard. She introduced herself as the A-Level instructor, Toni, and asked me to sign some papers. Then she pointed me in the direction of the locker rooms.

I was so nervous, I could not look at a single person. I changed, I dragged my dance bag back to the room, I found a space at the *barre*. And I began *plié*-ing as if my life depended on it.

It took me about five minutes to break a sweat. That was when I began calming down. I gazed around the room again. Most of the other kids were just chatting now. I heard names of hometowns, schools, teachers.

And then I heard someone say, "Juilliard."

But it wasn't the word itself that caught my attention. It was the voice that said it. A familiar voice.

I was at the height of an *arabesque*, my right leg extended backward, when I looked around to see who was speaking.

Quint Walter.

He was standing against a *barre* on the other side of the room, kicking his legs over his head while carrying on a conversation with a group of kids.

My *arabesque* collapsed. I had to clutch the *barre*.

Of course, Quint would pick that moment to see me.

"Jessi?" he called out.

"Hi," I said.

Quint lowered his leg and *jeté*d over to me. "How — what — you're in this too?"

"Uh-huh," I grunted. Why is talking to boys so hard? I mean, I used to know Quint so well (he was even my boyfriend, sort of) and *still* I felt tongue-tied.

"This is so cool," Quint said. "You've seen me dance and you convinced me to audition for Juilliard, but I have never seen you dance! Now I *know* you must be good!"

A gorgeous girl next to us started giggling. "Modest, aren't you?"

"I meant — well, you know —"

The girl giggled again and extended her hand to me. "Since he's obviously not going to introduce us, I'm Maritza Cruz."

"Jessi Ramsey," I said.

"Maritza's in my ballet class at Juilliard," Quint explained. "David Brailsford personally recruited us."

Maritza rolled her eyes. "He has told that to everyone in this room, everyone in the elevator, and a few sidewalk vendors on Broadway."

"Well, it's true!" Quint insisted.

I burst out laughing. Quint is the sweetest guy, and I know he doesn't mean to sound conceited. But he had changed since I last saw him. He used to be worried about his image. He hated it when neighborhood kids teased him about being a ballet dancer. Now he seemed so much more confident. And Maritza really had his number.

I wondered if she was his girlfriend.

They sure did seem close. And they looked perfect together. For one thing, they had matching turnout. (That means their feet point slightly outward instead of straight. As silly as it sounds, that's important for a dancer.) They're both tall too. Quint is maybe five feet eight, and Maritza looked almost that height.

Quint has coffee-brown skin, a shade lighter than mine. His features are open and friendly. Maritza is a bit paler, almost golden-hued, with raven-black hair pulled into a ponytail. Her eyes and smile are huge. I could just see them in a *pas de deux*.

No, I did not feel jealous. I still felt perfectly comfortable just *liking* Quint as a friend. Having a boyfriend isn't something I think about much.

Who has time?

"Everybody!" Toni called out. "Let's clear the door, please!"

Before she even finished the sentence, people by the door began clapping. A familiar, tall figure swept through them, smiling and shaking hands.

Me? I had to struggle to keep my jaw closed. David Brailsford is even more magnetic in person than he is onstage. He doesn't walk, he glides. His skin is a luscious deep brown, and his eyes seem to catch the light. "Welcome, everybody!" he called out in a deeeeeeep, loud voice with a slight West Indian accent. "Are you all ready to dance?"

"Yeeeaaaa!" we called out.

As Toni ushered the parents into the hallway, Mr. Brailsford asked us to sit around him in a semicircle.

"First, I want to thank you for accepting my

offer," Mr. Brailsford began. "I know some of you are far from home. I know how much your families had to sacrifice for you to come here. Perhaps some of you are even questioning if it's worth the trouble."

"If you want to be a pro, it is," said a boy with red hair.

Most of the class murmured in agreement.

"Well, you are indeed some of the finest young dancers I have seen," Mr. Brailsford said with a chuckle. "But if you're looking for professional training, you're in the wrong place."

That was not what I expected to hear. I could tell no one else did either.

"This class is about one thing." Mr. Brailsford held up a finger. "Love." Then he held up another. "And dance."

"That's two things," the red-haired boy said.

Mr. Brailsford brought the two fingers together. "Here, they're the same. This class is not about competition and pressure. You will not need to diet. You will not be graded. Your task is simple: to explore something you love to the utmost. With hard work. With joy. So that no matter what you become — a ballet star, a doctor, a fire chief — you will have had the dance experience of your life. An experience you will take with you always."

"All riiight!" shouted Quint.

Maritza started clapping. I joined her. Soon

the whole class was whistling and applauding with us.

Mr. Brailsford beamed at us. "Okay, now here's how we do it. Each day will be divided into three parts. Two of them are dance related: group dance class and individual instruction. During the first week you'll work mostly with Toni, as I circulate among the groups. I'll be teaching you individually next week. The last part of the day is academic tutorial. That's a fancy way of saying school. Your tutors are top-notch, and they'll be working you hard."

A groan went up from the room.

"But I've given them strict instructions: no homework on weekends!" Brailsford went on. "One more thing. On our last day, which is a Wednesday, we will be having an exhibition performance. You, the A-Level, will perform a group number choreographed by me. Now, everybody up for stretches."

I leaped to my feet. I, Jessi Ramsey, was going to be choreographed by the master. What a feeling.

But I couldn't think about that just then. Quint, Maritza, and I grabbed the *barre*.

The accompanist started playing. Toni stood in first position and announced, "Okay, watch me and *plié*!"

I was charged up. I felt as if I could do anything. I was going to be perfect.

As we began the warm-up, I saw Mr. Brailsford walking around the room. I couldn't wait for him to notice me. To stand next to me and admire me. He didn't have to tell me I was the next Gelsey Kirkland, just smile and nod. The way Mme Noelle does when I'm doing well in my regular ballet class.

Well, he stood next to me, all right. So did Toni. Many times. And they were both as nice as could be.

But each time, they corrected me.

My back was swayed. My arms were curved too much. My fingers were stiff. My fifth position was too wide.

This was nothing like Mme Noelle's class. It was nothing like Mme Noelle's warm-up, either. Mr. Brailsford was making us exercise muscles I didn't know existed.

Was he picking on Quint? On Maritza? Hardly at all.

Just me.

Was I that awful?

When Toni announced our first break, I was numb. I slumped out to the watercooler.

Maritza and Quint introduced me to some classmates. I tried to be friendly, but I barely registered their names.

"You looked great, Jessi," Maritza said.

"What am I doing here?" I blurted out. "I was a mistake!"

44

Quint gave me a funny look. "Say what?"

"At my audition, they probably accepted someone else, but they checked off my name by accident," I mumbled.

"I was thinking the same thing about myself!" exclaimed a girl named Celeste.

"Me too," Maritza said.

"But he hardly said a thing to you," I remarked.

"Sure he did," Maritza replied. "You were too busy concentrating to notice. He was on everybody's case. Even Baryshnikov over here." She gestured toward Quint.

Quint smiled. "Jessi, just relax. Remember, we're here to learn and have fun."

I took a deep breath. I choked back tears.

How was the rest of the day? Well, I survived. I did a few good pirouettes. I fell on a *piqué* turn and smashed into a mirror during a routine. Mr. Brailsford corrected me a thousand times, but he did say "Nice job" once. Although that might have been to the girl behind me.

By tutorials, I was a wreck. I couldn't pay attention. To add insult to injury, we were assigned homework.

Boy, was I happy to see Michael in the hallway at the end of the day. I grabbed my dance bag, called good-bye to my friends, and turned to leave.

"Wait!" Quint said, running to me. "So. You want to do something? Maybe not tonight, but maybe some other night? You know, like come over to my house for dinner?"

"Sure," I said.

"Great." Quint was backing down the hallway. "I mean, you'll see my family. They'll be so surprised. . . ."

"I'd like that."

"Great. Okay, 'bye." He nearly tripped over a dance bag. Grinning, he ran into the locker room.

"That guy is a *dancer*?" Michael asked as we headed toward the elevator.

I laughed. "He just has trouble walking."

"Ah, young love. It can make a clod of anyone."

"*Michael*! It's not like that at all. He has a girlfriend, anyway."

"Okay, okay," Michael said with a big smile. "Looks deceive, I guess."

As we entered the elevator, I could see Quint emerging from the locker room. He was grinning at me and waving.

I waved back.

I wasn't worried. Michael was being silly. That's all.

CHAPTER 5

Tuesday

This evening I baby-sat for Becca and Squirt. Jessi's been gone for two days, and Mrs. Ramsey had warned me that Becca was in a bad mood.

So I stocked my Kid-Kit with lots of stuff Becca and Squirt like. I promised myself I'd be gentle and understanding. I planned a few fun activities.

The more I think about it, maybe I shouldn't have taken the job in the first place. . . .

"Becca! Mallory's here!" Mama called into the house.

Mallory stepped inside, lugging her Kid-Kit.

Squirt came toddling into the room. When he saw Mallory, he began jumping up and down. "Maa-ree! Maa-ree!"

"Hi!" Mallory said, kneeling down to pick him up.

But Squirt just shot past her and climbed onto the armchair by the living room window. "Dess-see? Dess-see?"

"He's been doing that since yesterday," Mrs. Ramsey said with a sigh, "every time he sees something or someone that reminds him of Jessi."

Squirt turned around expectantly at the sound of the name. "Dess-see!"

"*Becca!*" Mama called again. "Come down and say hello!"

Mallory heard footsteps clomping downstairs. But it was Daddy, dressed up and ready to go to out. "Shhh," he said. "I think she's napping."

My parents gave Mallory instructions, kissed Squirt good-bye, and left.

Squirt watched them go. Then he slid off the chair and toddled away.

Mallory followed after him, pulling a picture book out of her Kid-Kit. "Want to read, Squirt?"

"No." Squirt went into the den and lay down on the floor.

Mallory felt around in her Kid-Kit for a few plastic trains she'd brought.

Upstairs she heard a loud thump.

Quickly she left the den, hooked shut the protective toddler fence, then darted up to Becca's bedroom and opened the door.

Becca's desk lamp was on. A sheet of crumpled-up loose-leaf paper and a math text-book lay on the floor.

Becca was in bed, her eyes closed.

"Are you awake?" Mallory asked.

Becca turned around to face the wall. "No."

"Having problems with homework?"

"I hate homework. I hate school. I hate you."

Mallory took a deep breath. She sat at the foot of Becca's bed.

Now, *I* would have gotten angry at Becca. I would have lectured her about respect or something like that. But Mal tried to follow Rule Number One of baby-sitting: Let the child talk problems out.

"You sound very unhappy," she said.

"So?" Becca replied.

"Is this about Jessi?"

"No."

"You miss her, don't you?"

"No."

Mallory shrugged. "I do."

"So go to New York stupid City."

"It's okay to miss someone, you know. It's okay to talk about it too."

"So talk about it."

Time for Rule Number Two: Know when to back off.

Mal stood up. "I should go downstairs and check on your brother. I brought Junior Monopoly and Guess Who, if you're interested."

"I'm not."

"Look, Becca. I know how you feel. If you come down, maybe we can write Jessi a letter."

"She has a phone."

"Okay. Want to call her instead?"

"Maybe."

Mallory darted back downstairs and into the den.

Squirt was standing by the sofa, leaning over, his forehead on the cushion.

"Hi, Squirt," Mal said, unhooking the fence.

Squirt lifted his head and looked at her dully. Then he toddled past the open fence and into the living room.

Back up onto the armchair he went, staring out the window.

(Honestly, I wish Mallory hadn't told me all this. I'm teary just thinking about it.)

50

Mal jumped onto the living room sofa and hid behind the throw pillows. "Uh-oh . . . where's Mallory?"

Hide-and-seek is Squirt's favorite game. Giggling, he ran to her and began pulling off the pillows.

"Boo!" Mallory said.

"Eeeeeee!" Squirt screamed happily.

"Quiet!" Becca grumbled, walking into the living room with a pad of drawing paper and a set of markers.

"Kay-o!" Squirt squealed. (Translation: *crayon*.)

"Guess what? I can draw the solar system, with all the planets," Becca said. "I learned yesterday. Jessi will be soooo surprised."

Zoom. Mallory went to fetch some crayons. Before long, the three of them were making art projects to send me. (They were great. I received a solar system that looked like orbiting basketballs; three pages full of scribbles, handprints, and smudges; and a fantastic portrait of Becca and Squirt.)

My brother and sister were very proud of their work. Mal was thrilled that they were showing signs of life.

"Can we fax these to her?" Becca asked excitedly. "The drugstore in town has a fax machine."

"Well, they're kind of large," Mallory said.

"And we don't know if Michael has a fax machine."

Becca jumped up. "Let's find out! Come on, Squirt, we're going to call Jessi!"

"*Dess-see!*" Squirt squealed.

Mallory followed Becca into the kitchen. Becca looked up Michael's number and tapped it out. Mallory pressed the speakerphone button so they could all listen.

It was about five-thirty. (That meant I was walking with Michael to a restaurant in Little Italy, where we met Marian for dinner.)

"Michael and Marian can't come to the phone," the answering machine crackled, "so please leave a message when you hear the tone."

Becca hung up.

"Didn't you want to say anything?" Mallory asked.

Becca shook her head. "We'll try later."

Well, they did try. Several times.

After the second try, Becca became all excited. She thought I'd left Brooklyn and was coming home.

After the fourth, she began thinking I'd been kidnapped.

After the sixth, she was convinced that I was actually there but refusing to take calls.

Becca left a message on the seventh try. Which, of course, was the one Michael, Marian, and I heard that night when we returned to the apartment.

"I hate you and I hope you never come back."

I called home right after hearing that.

But Becca was already asleep. So I chatted with Mama and Daddy, then called Mallory's house.

She was asleep too. Her mom said she'd had a long, long day.

CHAPTER 6

"*Chassé* left, *echappé, boureé* with *port de bras, arabesque, assemble, assemble* . . . Okay, this is it, kids: *pirouette* and *pas de chat* into a *tour jeté* around the room!"

Toni's voice echoed loudly over the piano music. But I wasn't really listening. The steps were already burned into my brain. We'd been practicing them with Toni all Wednesday morning.

Now Mr. Brailsford himself was watching. Out of the corner of my eye I could see him swaying to the music and smiling.

I was leaping higher than I ever had. And working harder. Sweat was flinging off me with each spin.

"And *stop!*" Toni yelled as the pianist played the last chords.

I landed in third position, my arms extended. My chest was heaving. The panting in the room sounded like plank-sawing in wood shop.

"Yyyyyes!" shouted Mr. Brailsford. "You kids are cooking! Take a break!"

I dropped my arms and grabbed my towel from the floor. Patting my forehead, I walked into the hallway.

"Jessica?" Mr. Brailsford called out.

I spun around. "Me?"

"How long have you been dancing?" he asked.

Uh-oh.

He was kicking me out.

He had found the mistake on the audition acceptance sheet.

"Um, well, I'm eleven and I've been taking classes with Madame Noelle — she's in Stamford — but I started before that, in Oakley, which is in New Jersey, and that was when I was three, I think, or maybe it was after my fourth birthday, so I guess eight or seven and a half years, something like that."

Did I sound nervous? I was petrified.

Mr. Brailsford nodded. "You have great style, Jessica. Extraordinary lift. A real Judith Jamison quality."

"*Me?*"

Is there a word for a mirage of the ears? That's what I thought was happening. Judith Jamison is only the most legendary African-American ballerina who ever lived.

"Keep up the good work," Mr. Brailsford

said. "Just make sure not to arch your back so much on those *jetés*."

"Sure," I squeaked.

Toni drew Mr. Brailsford away with some questions. I *jeté*d into the hallway with a perfect back.

Quint and Maritza were waiting for me. "What'd he say?" Maritza asked.

"*He. Likes. Me!*" I blurted out. "He said I remind him of Judith Jamison."

"Cool!" Quint said.

Maritza gave me a hug. "I knew it!"

The rest of the day, I was flying. Even tutorials went well.

At the end of the day, Maritza introduced me to a tall, stunning girl in the hallway. "Jessi, this is my sister, Tanisha. She's in the full-time program. It's for future professionals."

Tanisha was very nice. I told her my story, and she said, "Girl, I'd be on cloud nine if I were you."

I was. When Michael arrived to pick me up, I told him every detail. I could not stop talking.

We rode the elevator down with Maritza and Tanisha. We gabbed through the lobby. We gabbed up Broadway. We gabbed walking down the subway steps.

Somewhere in the midst of the gabbing, I found out that Maritza and Tanisha lived in Brooklyn Heights. When Maritza mentioned the address, Michael said it was within walking distance of his apartment.

This was my lucky day.

"Want to come over?" Maritza and I both said at the same time.

"My house first," Maritza said. "I'll call my friends. You'll love them."

I turned to Michael. "Can I? Please?"

"Mom and Dad won't mind," Tanisha said. "We were going to order in pizza today anyway."

Michael shrugged. "Leftovers at our house. You win."

We thanked Michael and started gabbing again. I loved having someone to gab with on the subway. The atmosphere during rush hour is so boring.

The moment we walked inside the Cruzes' apartment, Maritza started making phone calls to her friends. I sat at the kitchen table with Tanisha and munched on pretzels.

Tanisha told me that some of the full-time students tour with Dance New York. She described a standing ovation in Italy. She showed me an award the Dance New York members had received from the mayor of San Francisco. She played a videotape of a performance she was in that was broadcast coast-to-coast on public television.

I was completely blown away. "How hard is

it to be accepted to the full-time program?"

"Very," Tanisha said. "It's unbelievably hard work too. All that stuff Mr. Brailsford told you about no competition? Forget it. You are on a track. A couple of dancers eventually make it into the company. A few others do Broadway shows or teach. Everyone else . . ." She shrugged and her voice drifted away.

BZZZZZZT!

Maritza jumped up from the table. "That's Rasheen. He lives down the hall."

One by one, Maritza's friends began arriving.

Rasheen was a techno whiz who brought over a fancy camcorder. He seemed nice, but he hardly ever took his face away from the viewfinder.

Next came Simi, who lived around the corner. She didn't know a thing about ballet, but whenever Maritza and I would dance for the camcorder, she would join in. With a straight face, she would turn our delicate *pas de deux* into comedy routines.

Quint came over too (his mom was in Brooklyn to have dinner with friends, so he was able to come in from Manhattan). Then kids named Brandon, Julissa, and Denise arrived.

My little visit had turned into a pizza party. Mr. and Mrs. Cruz were awfully nice about it. They just ordered extra food. They even mugged for the video.

I hadn't laughed so hard in a long time. Since my last Baby-sitters Club meeting, really.

But this was different.

I tried to think of the last time I'd been in a room full of African-American friends. Not since my family lived in Oakley.

Now, I love my Stoneybrook friends. And I absolutely hate all forms of racism. But I couldn't help the way I was feeling. Being with Maritza's friends was so . . . refreshing.

We polished off three large pizzas and tons of soda. We watched Rasheen's video and laughed our heads off.

Around eight, everyone started leaving. Rasheen and Simi walked home. The others were collected by their parents.

Quint and I were the only ones remaining. When his mom buzzed on the intercom, he began putting on his down coat and his hat. "This was fun," he said, giving me a big smile.

"Yeah," I said. "I love Maritza's friends."

"Oh, I almost forgot. How's Saturday? For coming over to my house?"

"Um, well, I'll ask my cousin."

"My family can't wait to see you again. Especially Morgan and Tyler. They love you. My mom and dad too. They call you the Dance Angel because you were the one who made me go to Juilliard."

"I didn't make you! You auditioned."

"Dad always says, 'Behind every successful man, there's a good woman.' " Quint laughed. "Mom hates that. She says, 'And vice versa!' I guess it's true both ways, huh?"

I smiled and nodded. But I did not feel terribly comfortable. Quint was acting too friendly. Almost flirtatious. And Maritza was right behind us.

Fortunately, Mrs. Walter rang the doorbell a moment later. As she and Quint left she repeated the invitation.

Now I was the only guest left. Maritza and Tanisha were cleaning up the kitchen, so I pitched in. I didn't know whether or not to mention anything about the way Quint was acting.

Tanisha beat me to it. "You pick them well, Jessi."

"Pick?" I repeated.

Tanisha nodded. "He's cute."

I darted a nervous glance toward Maritza. "Well, uh, it's not — I mean, a long time ago we — but —"

Maritza gave me a curious glance. "He *is* your boyfriend, isn't he?"

"No!" I shot back. "He used to be, sort of, I guess. But we're just friends, that's all. I thought he was *your* boyfriend."

"What on earth gave you that idea?" Maritza burst out laughing.

"I don't know. You seem close —"

"We've been in class together since kindergarten," Maritza explained. "Don't you worry. He's free."

"Not for long," Tanisha said. "Not with Jessi around."

I shook my head. "No! I mean, I don't want a boyfriend. I like Quint and all, but that's not what I had in mind."

"Have you told *him* that?" Maritza asked.

"Should I? Do you think I need to?"

Maritza and Tanisha exchanged a Look.

"I guess you'll find out on Saturday," Maritza said.

CHAPTER 7

"So, Jessi's doing these *piqué* turns, right?" Quint said, waving a forkful of pork roast in the air. "And —"

"Wait. What's P. K.?" Mr. Walter asked.

"Pretty Complicated," said Quint's six-year-old sister, Morgan.

Quint's brother, Tyler, let out a big groan. (He's nine.) "That would be P. C., dumbhead."

"Don't call your sister names," Mrs. Walter scolded.

"*Piqué*, not P.K.," Quint barreled on. "It's French for these spins where you have to kick. Anyway, Jessi's doing them, okay? And Mr. Brailsford walks by, and he gets it smack on the rear end!"

Mr. Walter gave a big belly laugh. Tyler and Morgan were howling.

Me? I was covering my face with my hand. "Did you *have* to mention that?"

"And Maritza says, 'She'll never wash that toe shoe again!' " Quint went on.

Another burst of laughter. Except from Mrs. Walter, who calmly asked, "Some more yams, Jessi?"

I really like the Walters. Even though they were all laughing at my expense. It was a gentle, friendly kind of teasing. They loved to rib each other too. The atmosphere around the table was warm and comfortable.

Until Quint put his arm around the back of my chair. "Mr. Brailsford didn't mind," he said. "He knows Jessi's the best in the class."

"No way," I retorted.

Quint was grinning. He leaned his face close to mine. "You are so modest."

"Ooooooh," Morgan said, looking at us with a mischievous glint in her eye. She leaned toward Tyler and started whispering.

Now, I liked being the center of attention. And it really did feel great to be with the Walters again.

But my suspicions about Quint were increasing. Did he really think we'd gone back in time? Had he forgotten the talk we'd had, about being just friends?

It sure looked like it.

How could I have been so stupid? I never should have agreed to come over. I mean, *din-*

ner with the family? That was pretty serious. When he asked me, I should have suggested something more casual, like an afternoon walk in the park.

No. I couldn't have done that. Mr. Brailsford had taken all of us students to a Saturday morning rehearsal of Dance New York and then a long lunch at a fancy restaurant.

Even there, Quint had been glued to my side. And Maritza had kept shooting me meaningful looks. But I hadn't said a thing to Quint.

Well, honestly, what could I have said?

"Sorry, I can't come over tonight because I think you might have the wrong idea in mind?"

"Quint, even though we're among all these people, let's talk about our relationship?"

No way.

Okay. I would talk to Quint. Later. In the meantime, I was going to enjoy the company and the dinner.

I changed the topic of conversation. I asked Tyler and Morgan about school. I asked Mr. Walter about his job. (That was a mistake. He's a chemical engineer, and I couldn't understand a word he said.)

After dinner, Morgan insisted on showing me some gymnastics moves. And Tyler just had to play his newest video game with me.

Quint seemed impatient. A few minutes into the video game, he said, "Uh, Tyler? She's not *that* interested in computers."

"I love them," I quickly said.

Finally Quint asked, "Why don't you and I take a walk? There's a great place for desserts and stuff, with booths. It's really private."

I looked at my watch. It was nine o'clock. "Uh-oh. Michael wanted me home by now."

"I'll take you there!" Quint quickly offered.

"To Brooklyn?"

"I love subway rides."

"Well, Michael gave me cab fare. Maybe another time."

Okay, so I didn't talk to him. I chickened out.

I promised myself I'd do it some other time.

Soon.

I could hear the sad, low tones of a cello as I approached Marian and Michael's apartment. It was so beautiful, I didn't want to walk in and interrupt.

I turned the key softly and let myself in.

Immediately Marian stopped playing. "Hi, Jessi."

"Keep going," I said. "I didn't know you played."

Michael peered in from the kitchen. "She used to play professionally."

"Semi," Marian corrected him. "I was in a lo-cal orchestra during college. But never mind that. How was your dinner?"

"Fun, I guess," I said, plopping myself down on the sofa. "But I'm afraid Michael was right about Quint."

"I won't say I told you so," Michael called out. "But I did."

"Shush," Marian called back, then leaned to-ward me. "So Quint's interested, but you just want to be friends."

I nodded. "All day long I wanted to say something to him, but I didn't."

"Has he actually told you how he feels?" Marian asked.

"No," I replied. "That's what makes it hard. I mean, what if I'm wrong? What if he's just af-fectionate with everybody? He didn't used to be that way, but he's changed a lot since I last saw him. He's much more outgoing."

Marian nodded understandingly. "You don't want to presume. It would be embarrassing to have a big talk with him, only to find out that he *wasn't* trying to be serious after all."

Michael came in, drying his hands with a dish towel. "I thought Marian hated me for years. I used to sit through all those boring classical music concerts just to get a glimpse of her. Just hoping she'd notice me."

"You *loved* those concerts!" Marian protested.

"Nah, I just loved the first-chair cellist," Michael said with a grin.

"You met in college?" I asked.

"I was at the New England Conservatory," Marian said. "And Michael was at the Massachusetts College of Art —"

Bleeeeeep! went the phone.

Michael ran into the kitchen to answer. "It's for you, Jessi!" he announced. "Maritza. She called earlier too."

I excused myself and took the call. "Hello?"

"Well?" was Maritza's greeting. "Did you tell him?"

"With his family around?"

"Good point. He didn't try to kiss you or anything, did he?"

"No. He hasn't even said he likes me. I'm so confused, Maritza. What am I going to do? Should I wait for him to tell me how he feels? Or should I say something first, even though I'm not totally sure?"

"Okay. Okay. My brain is hatching a plan. If you want to talk to him, you should be around people who care about you. Right? So. All my friends really want to get to know you better. How about if I invite them over, plus you and Quint. If you want to talk to him, great. We'll make sure no one bothers you, but we'll be around in case you need us. If you don't talk to him, that's fine too."

"But we're all taking a backstage tour at Lincoln Center tomorrow."

"Okay. Afterward, then. My house. Deal?"

"Deal."

Maritza is so smart.

We talked awhile longer. Marian started playing again, so after I hung up, I listened. I had the urge to call Mallory and ask her opinion about my dilemma, but it was awfully late and I was tired.

I said good night at the end of a Bach cello sonata and slumped off to my room.

A few minutes later, after I had washed up, I was lying in bed, admiring the abstract artwork on the walls. The paintings had such vivid colors in interesting combinations.

I'm no Claudia Kishi. I don't really understand modern art. But I know when I like something. And I liked this.

I'd been in Brooklyn a week now, and each night I felt I was seeing something different on the walls. That first depressing day, the paintings seemed gloomy. When I'd been excited, the paintings seemed exuberant and happy. Now, thinking about Quint, I found the artwork to be edgy, questioning. With hidden shapes.

I heard footsteps in the hall. I climbed out of bed, opened my door, and peeked out.

It was Michael.

"Hi. Who did these paintings?"

Michael winced. "Do you hate them? Sorry. I did them when I was a student."

"I *love* them, Michael. You are so talented. You could have been a pro."

"You sound like my mom," Michael said with a chuckle. "She's still mad that I didn't become an artist. When I told her I was going to business school, I thought she was going to disown me."

"Why would she be *mad*? You have such a nice life. And you're happy. Aren't you?"

"I suppose. I didn't want to starve — which I might have done if I had become an artist. But my mom really wanted me to live out my dream, Jessi. She wanted Marian to do the same." Michael shrugged. "And we didn't."

Live out your dream. Aunt Cecelia had said that to me too. I never paid much attention to it. I guess that's because of the annoying way she said it.

"My mom," Michael added with a half smile, "can be hard to please. I sure hope you get along with her better than I ever did."

"I try," I said.

"Look at it this way. If I were an artist, you might be staying in some cold, cramped downtown walk-up, surrounded by the smells of acrylic paint and turpentine."

I laughed. We said good night again and I went back to bed.

As I dozed off, my mind was swirling. Not about Quint, or Dance New York, or David Brailsford. I was thinking about Claudia, back home in Stoneybrook, trapped in a family of achievers. They support her, more or less, but frankly, if she grew up to do Michael's kind of work, they'd be thrilled.

In my family, the opposite was true. My aunt, stuffy old Cecelia, had an artistic soul.

Who'd have thought it?

CHAPTER 8

"Lift! *Li-i-i-ift!* Yes! Nice work, Jessica!"

Normally no one calls me Jessica. I tell everyone I prefer Jessi. The only exceptions are people I'm too afraid to correct — my parents, my teachers, and Aunt Cecelia, usually when they're angry.

I'd just added one name to that list.

David Brailsford.

Even after a full week, I was in awe whenever he walked into the room. It was kind of like Zeus descending from Mount Olympus.

But one-on-one, personal, private instruction?

He could call me Myrtle and I wouldn't protest.

During my first week, almost all of my individual instruction had been with Toni. She was an excellent teacher, very supportive and funny. Occasionally, Mr. Brailsford would drop in, but just to make a few comments.

This week, he was giving us his full attention.

"Okay, you're dropping your left shoulder a bit on that *pirouette*," he said.

"I always do that," I said with a sigh.

"You can change," Mr. Brailsford said. "Where there's a will, there's a way. Let's try it again."

I *pirouetted*. This time my right shoulder dipped.

But I did not wait for a comment. I went right into a double *pirouette*, which I was determined to do perfectly.

Instead, I went around three times.

A *perfect* triple. Which I'd never, ever been able to do in my life.

Mr. Brailsford applauded. "*Excellent!* Where did *that* come from?"

I couldn't stop giggling. "I can't believe I did that."

"Believe it. It will be the first of many, Jessica. You're showing terrific improvement. Okay, let's do the piece Toni taught you, from the top."

Nice work.

Excellent.

Terrific improvement.

The compliments were burning themselves into my memory. Three good ones, right in a row.

I wanted our session to last forever. I was having the best time.

When it was over, I danced out of the room.

I nearly stepped on Quint. He was doing stretches on the floor.

"Don't tell me," he said with a big smile. "Mr. Brailsford wants you to be in his next ballet."

"No, not quite," I said, calmly walking toward the vending machine.

"He wants to promote you to D-Level."

"Nope."

"I heard him say you were excellent," Quint said, hopping up from the floor.

"You have good ears."

"No. He just has a loud voice. Anyway, I'm sure you were as great as usual, Ms. Star of the Future."

Remember the Big Talk that Quint and I were supposed to have on Sunday? Well, guess what? It didn't happen.

We were too busy. First of all, we used Rasheen's camcorder to make a horror video called *Ballet Is Murder*, which I directed. After that I led a game of charades. Then I choreographed a few karaoke numbers.

No Talk.

Afterward, Maritza told me, "No problem. Just don't lead him on. If he sees you smiling too much or responding to his jokes, he might get the wrong impression."

I didn't totally agree. I wasn't going to be

cold. Not to someone as nice as Quint. I was determined to be polite but just a little distant. Friendly but not *girl*friendly.

Simple. He'd get the message.

Now Quint was standing right next to me, his arm up against the vending machine.

"Excuse me," I said, ducking into the practice room to fetch my dance bag.

I took out my wallet and searched around for money for the machine.

Quint was right behind me. "I'll treat," he volunteered.

I pulled out a dollar bill of my own, just in time. "No, thanks."

"Hey, girl!" called Maritza from down the hallway. "How'd it go?"

I whirled away from the machine and ran toward her.

"It was soooo great," I said. "At first I didn't think I could move. I mean, there he was." I imitated Mr. Brailsford's big grin and deepened my voice. " 'Jessicaaaa, you must lo-o-o-ower your left shoulder.' My heart was pumping so fast, I couldn't even talk. I tried to do a double *pirouette* but I went around three times without thinking and he said, 'E-e-excel-lent. Where did thaaaaat come from?' "

Maritza was not laughing. She was looking at something over my shoulder. So was Quint.

I turned around to see Mr. Brailsford leaning against the doorjamb of the practice room.

"We-e-e-ell, an actress as well as a balleri-naaaa!" he bellowed, in an imitation of my imitation of his voice.

I nearly melted into the floor. "Sorry!" I squeaked, burying my head in my hands.

Mr. Brailsford burst out laughing. "No offense taken. I appreciate all kinds of talent."

Another student was walking into the practice room just then. Mr. Brailsford waved good-bye and closed the door behind them.

I collapsed slowly to the carpet. "Oh, great. Last week I kicked him. This week I made fun of him."

Quint knelt beside me. "Hey, don't worry. He was amused."

"He's going to expel me," I replied.

Quint was about to put his arm around me, but Maritza managed to wedge herself between us. "Jessi, it's lunchtime. You need to take a walk. To clear your head. Come on."

We headed down the corridor, chatting. Out of the corner of my eye I could see Quint hesitating, trying to decide whether or not to go with us. Finally he just stayed put.

"Maritza," I said, "aren't we being a little snobby? We could have invited him."

"Mr. Brailsford?"

"No. Quint."

"Hey, you two!" called Tanisha, who was waiting near the elevator. "Ready to eat?"

We rode down the elevator and walked outside without our coats. We let the cold January air shock us as we darted to the deli at the end of the block. The deli smelled heavenly, like hot soup and pot roast.

My mood was lifting again. Slightly.

As Tanisha ordered our sandwiches, Maritza and I picked out cartons of juice.

"He must think I hate him," I said.

"Quint?" Maritza asked.

"No. Mr. Brailsford."

"Jessi, your imitation wasn't cruel. He's a grown man. He can take it. You heard how he laughed."

"I guess." I sighed. "But you're right about Quint. He's probably furious at me."

"Furious at *me*. I was the one who sat between you two."

I laughed. "You know, you didn't have to do that. He's not a wild monster."

"No, just wild with lo-o-o-o-ove."

Tanisha turned toward us from the sandwich counter. "Honey, he's a good-looking guy. Often the cute ones don't like strong women. Obviously he does — because he likes you, Jessi. You should think twice about passing him up."

I loved the way Tanisha was talking to me. It

made me feel at least fifteen. But I wasn't sure she understood the situation.

"I'm not that strong. Mr. Brailsford told me I need to work on my jumps and do push-ups —"

"I don't mean strong *dancer*. I mean strong *woman*," Tanisha said. "You were chewing the scenery at that party yesterday."

That is such a funny expression. It means *hogging the stage*. Until then, though, I'd never heard anyone use it to describe me.

"It's true, Jessi," Maritza agreed. "You hardly know my friends, and you had them running around as if you were their camp counselor. And they loved every minute of it."

"Ya sangwiches, goils?" called the man behind the counter, in the strongest New York accent I have ever heard.

Maritza and Tanisha practically exploded with laughter. They had to cover their mouths.

I was laughing too. But not at the accent.

I was just plain happy. About my fabulous new life.

Me, Jessi Ramsey. Not only a ballerina acclaimed by David Brailsford, but yes, ladies and gentlemen, a Born Leader too.

At last I had something to tell Kristy.

Monday was just the beginning of a dream-come-true week. Mr. Brailsford was really taking an interest in me. He didn't push me to do the impossible, but he never let me settle for less than my best. A word, an image, a slight adjustment in body position — he knew just how to make me change.

Some of my best times were after practice. Michael and Marian took me to hear jazz at the Blue Note (Tuesday), to a Broadway show (Thursday), and to a concert at Carnegie Hall (Friday), plus a few fantastic restaurants. On Wednesday I saw a movie with Maritza and her friends.

Homework? I did it on my subway rides, during breaks, whenever. I felt so alive and alert, I never had trouble concentrating.

As for Quint and me, well, things stayed pretty much the same. He did ask me to his house for dinner Friday night, but I couldn't go because of the concert. And during the day we were always — *always* — surrounded by a crowd.

On Friday I noticed he looked kind of quiet. So I asked him if everything was okay.

He just smiled and shrugged. "Fine."

"Are you sure?"

"Uh-huh."

"Okay," I said, turning back to the practice room.

"Jessi," he called out.

"What?" I said.

"That's the most you've said to me all week."

"I'm sorry! I wasn't, like, insinuating anything. Just being friendly in a normal way. You know, not any different from anyone else —"

Quint laughed. "What I mean is, we've all been so busy. What a week, huh?"

"Amazing," I replied.

Whew. False alarm.

I was beginning to think my problem might not be much of a problem at all.

When Michael, Marian, and I arrived home from the concert on Friday, we found a message from Maritza on the answering machine. Her parents wanted to treat her whole group of friends to a "New York Saturation Saturday" — Statue of Liberty, Twin Towers, Chinatown, Rockefeller Center skating rink, and dinner in Little Italy.

I called my parents right away and asked if I could stay in New York for another weekend.

Daddy agreed, but Mama sounded a little reluctant. "Becca was expecting to see you," she said. "Mallory too."

Oops.

"Can I talk to Becca?"

"She's sleeping."

"I'll call tomorrow and explain."

We said good-bye. Then I tried Mallory.

She was very quiet when I told her what had happened. "Oh," she said. "Okay."

Ugh. She was mad.

An idea hit me. "I know. Why don't you come here next weekend?"

"Could I?"

I looked at Michael and Marian. They both nodded. "Yup," I said.

"I'll work on Mom and Dad," Mallory said.

Done.

I knew this was going to work.

Where there's a will, there's a way.

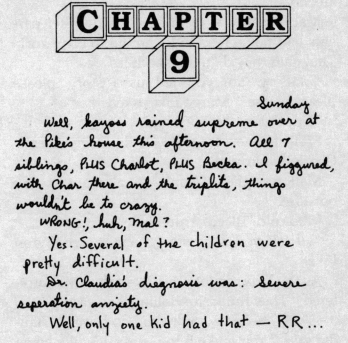

CHAPTER 9

Sunday

Well, kayoss rained supreme over at the Pike's house this afternoon. All 7 siblings, PLUS Charlot, PLUS Becka. I figgured, with Char there and the triplits, things wouldn't be to crazy.

WRONG!, huh, Mal?

Yes. Several of the children were pretty difficult.

Dr. Claudia's diegnosis was: Severe seperation anziety.

Well, only one kid had that — RR...

The RR, of course, is Rebecca Ramsey.

But Mallory wasn't telling the whole truth. Becca was not the only one with separation anxiety.

Mal herself was feeling pretty low. Her parents had not agreed to let her go to New York. They said they'd "think about it."

"Mallory, can you tell us a story, please please please?" Margo Pike asked.

"Not today," Mallory said.

"Tell us one about the Oogly Oogly Beast!" Charlotte pleaded.

Mallory sighed. "Don't you all want to play outside?"

"Too cold," Becca grumbled.

"*I'll* tell you all a story," announced Byron Pike.

As the kids ran into the Pikes' den, Mal muttered, "They think storytelling is so easy."

"That's because you're so good at it," Claudia said. "You make it look easy. It's like when I show Janine my art. She shrugs it off. She calls it play therapy."

Mal nodded silently.

"Jessi too," Claudia rambled on. "She does those spin things like they're nothing."

"Pirouettes," Mallory said.

"Whatever. Anyway, I tried one and nearly destroyed my ankle."

"Well, she's doing a lot of them this weekend, I guess. That's why she can't be here."

Claudia's heart went out to Mal. She immediately thought about how lonely she had felt when she was first sent back to seventh grade.

"Come on, let's do something fun," she said, taking Mallory's hand.

Claudia dragged Mal to the den, where the Pike triplets were standing before an audience of six kids.

The triplets — Byron, Adam, and Jordan — are ten years old. They like to think they're too old for baby-sitters, so we treat them as helpers (and sometimes they even earn that title). The next oldest Pike is Vanessa (she's nine), then Nicky (eight), Margo (seven), and Claire (five).

Charlotte, by the way, is Becca's best friend. Like Becca, she's eight and very smart. (Unlike Becca, she's very quiet.)

"Okay, so, like, there was once this big spaceship that landed on a planet," Byron began.

"What planet?" Margo asked.

"I don't know, but it had lots of sand," Byron replied. "Anyway, these two robots were on it? Only one talked but the other didn't? But the one that didn't had this video inside that showed like a hologram or whatever in the air, and it was of this princess named, um, Princess Leda. And she was in trouble because her spaceship was being attacked by —"

Vanessa groaned. "That's just the *Star Wars* story with different names. Can't you think of something better?"

"I want to tell one!" Claire shouted, leaping up. "Um, this robot? He was little? He had this squeaky voice?"

"Ooh! Ooh! I know!" Adam blurted out.

"No robots," Nicky said.

Claire's face collapsed. *"No fair!"*

"Bo-ring!" Becca called out.

"I have a great one!" Adam protested. "It's, like, a real story, by Hans Christian Andersen. Called 'The Little Matchmaker.' "

"Waaaaaah!" cried Claire, running for the door.

Mallory scooped her up and hugged her. "It's 'The Little Match Girl,' and you interrupted Claire."

"She interrupted *me*!" Adam said.

"You're supposed to help, dork brain!" Jordan spoke up.

"I'm rubber, you're glue —" Adam began.

"Okay, everyone outside!" Mallory shouted. "I don't care how cold it is. Just put on your coats and play. Now!"

Mallory never talks like that. Claire was covering her ears.

The other kids seemed kind of shocked. They left the den. Mallory set Claire down so she could join them.

"*You* try amusing these kids," Adam the Seasoned Sitter murmured on his way out.

Claudia just stood there for a moment, not knowing what to say. But Mal swept by her and into the kitchen.

The kids were in the mud room, putting on their coats. Well, all except Becca, who was sitting at the table, staring out the window.

"Aren't you going outside?" Claudia asked.

"No," Becca said.

Mallory didn't seem to be moving outside either, so Claudia grabbed her coat. She remembered she had a few candy bars inside her coat pocket. "Hungry?" she asked.

"Nope," said Mallory and Becca at the same time.

"Maybe you guys can give Jessi a call," Claudia suggested.

"She's out," Mallory said. "Touring New York City."

"Besides, she doesn't want to talk to us," Becca added.

Claudia let out a sigh. "Well, don't have too much fun while I'm gone."

Frustrated, she stepped outside.

All the kids were gathered around Adam now, giggling and screaming. The Pikes' dog, Pow, was running around them, his tail wagging furiously. Adam was holding out a handheld tape recorder, shouting, "Stop! Let me make an introduction! Um, ladies and gentle-men, this is WPIKE, bringing you a day in the life of the Pikes!"

"WOOOOOOO!" shouted Margo into the mike.

Brrrrrup, burped Nicky.

ROWF! barked Pow.

"Bad idea!" yelled Byron. "This isn't work-ing."

That's when Claudia had an idea of her own.

Becca and Mal were feeling gloomy and lonely. The kids were wild. Everyone needed a project.

"*YYYYO!*" Claudia shouted, in her best Kristy Thomas voice. "Who wants to send a cassette telegram to Jessi?"

"MEEEEEEEE!"

Ta-da. Instant success. Everyone ran back in-side.

Mallory and Becca brightened a little at the suggestion.

"Maybe we can sing a song," Becca said.

"Good idea," Mallory agreed. "While you do that, let's make an order of presentation, so everyone can have a turn."

They all gathered around Mal, who had grabbed a pen and pad of paper from the kitchen desk.

"I'll tell about my class's rabbit!" Claire blurted out.

"Does Jessi like Game Boy?" Nicky asked.

"I want to read her my English report," Byron said.

"You'll put her to sleep," Adam said.

Mallory laughed. "One at a time, guys."

Claudia the Miracle Worker saves the day.

The tape, I have to say, was a work of genius. I still crack up whenever I listen to it.

CHAPTER 10

"I think it's totally unfair," said Marcus Glover.

"Who does he think we are?" Celeste Rodriguez chimed in. "Babies?"

"This could have been a perfect opportunity," complained Michiko Nakamura.

"It's not like we don't deserve it," added Randy Hamill.

The honeymoon was over.

Mr. Brailsford was no longer perfect. At least among the members of Dance New York Youth, A-Level.

This honeymoon had lasted a long time. It was already Tuesday of our third week. Only a week and a day were left in our session.

I was already starting to feel sad. Everyone I'd met was so great. I felt as if I'd been in a long, wonderful dream.

My classmates and I were having lunch at the SoHo Szechuan Chinese restaurant. Earlier,

Mr. Brailsford had announced the program for our exhibition performance.

The good news was, some of his famous friends from the dance world were going to be there. So was a reviewer from a major newspaper.

The bad news was, only upper-level students were going to have solos. No one in A-Level. All we were performing was our group ballet. "You don't need the pressure," Mr. Brailsford had announced. "Remember, we're here to learn and enjoy."

I was disappointed at first, but I got over it.

Some of my friends hadn't.

"At Juilliard, I get to do solos," Quint groused.

I grabbed a forkful of cold sesame noodles from a lazy Susan. "Well, I think Mr. Brailsford is right."

"If anyone should have a solo, it should be *you*, Jessi," Maritza said.

"Please. If I were doing a solo, I'd be a wreck. I sure wouldn't be here right now. I'd be at the *barre* — practicing, perfecting my solo, worrying. I don't want that. I'm having a great time doing just what we're doing."

"But it's good to have a goal," Marcus insisted.

"The group number is our goal," I said. "Look, just imagine if we were competing against each other with solos. Would we be sitting here together, all relaxed and happy?"

Quint nodded. "She has a point."

"Maybe," Marcus grumbled.

Michiko made a face. "Marcus Glover, Applause Lover."

Marcus looked warily around, then threw a piece of sweet-and-sour shrimp at her.

"Food fight!" Randy said, picking up a baby corn.

"Now *this* is competition," Celeste remarked.

Don't worry. No one else threw any food. For one thing, the head waiter was eyeing us now. For another, we were all laughing too hard.

We quickly finished up and paid our bill. It was warm for January, and a bright midday sun lit up the canyon of Broadway as we returned to the studio.

Everyone else was walking in pairs, slowly and lazily. I was alone. I closed my eyes for a moment and tilted my face toward the sun.

"Nice day, huh?"

Quint had joined me.

"Beautiful," I said.

"So . . . how about this Friday? For dinner, I mean. Have you made plans yet?"

"Uh . . . well, I'm waiting to hear if my friend Mal is visiting."

"*Mal?*" Quint's face fell. "A guy?"

"No. Mallory Pike."

"Oh. Right. I remember her. Cool. But what if she doesn't come?"

"I don't know, Quint —"

"I know what you mean. Maybe we should go out instead. Like to a movie or something. We could even go with other people. Like another couple. Or what about Thursday, or even Sunday —?"

Enough is enough, I said to myself. I could no longer ignore this.

"Quint," I said firmly. "We have to talk."

"We are talking," Quint said with a smile.

I glanced up the street. My classmates were ahead of us, chattering away.

Quint and I stopped walking. We were in a little nook formed by the back of a subway entrance and the brick wall of a building.

I looked at my watch. We still had about ten minutes before we had to return.

"What do you think we are?" I asked.

Quint laughed. "Is this a quiz? Let's see . . . talented. Coordinated. Funny. Black. Eleven going on twelve —"

"No, I mean, *we* we. You and me together. We're, like, *friends*, right?"

"That's what *I* thought," Quint said with a shrug.

"Because that's how we left things, remember? We were going to be long-distance friends, nothing more."

91

Quint nodded. "Sure I remember."

Whew.

"Great," I said. "That's all I wanted to know."

"Why are you asking me this, Jessi?"

"I don't know. I thought I was picking up these . . . strange vibes from you."

"You think I'm being strange?" Now Quint looked upset.

"I didn't mean it that way. Just like . . . oh, this is so embarrassing. I thought, maybe you wanted us to be . . . you know, a couple. That you were going back on our agreement."

"But I never did that."

"I know."

"I mean, when you were in Stoneybrook, I stopped calling you all the time."

"I know you did."

"I didn't beg you to visit anymore."

"I know."

"So we were long-distance friends," Quint said.

"Right. Look, I'm sorry —"

"And now we're not long-distance anymore."

Thunk.

I hadn't looked at it from that point of view.

"So, you think we're . . . automatically the way we used to be?"

Quint looked away. "Well, not *automatically*.

Not the way you've been acting to me. But I thought maybe you might . . . I mean, you're here. I *am* the same guy."

His voice was becoming smaller and smaller. When he said that last sentence he sounded like a little boy.

"Of course you are, Quint —"

"Did I do something wrong?"

"No. This really doesn't have anything to do with you. It's me. I don't want a boyfriend in my life right now. That's all. That's why I want us to be friends."

"Sorry." Quint nodded sadly. "I guess I didn't understand."

"It's my fault. I should have mentioned it earlier."

Quint took a deep breath. "I shouldn't have assumed."

"I didn't really give you reason not to, I guess."

"Jessi?"

"What?"

"When do you think you *will* be ready for a boyfriend?"

I shrugged. "Maybe when I'm thirteen? Fourteen? I don't know."

"Two years? Cool."

As we began walking back to the Dance New York building together, Quint was definitely different. Vibeless. I felt so relieved.

I could not wait to tell Maritza what had happened.

"Hey, will you at least let me say hi to Mallory?" Quint asked.

"Of course!" I said.

Just then I realized something strange. I hadn't mentioned a word about Quint to Mal yet. Usually *she's* the one I confide in about personal stuff.

But for nearly three weeks I'd been confiding in Maritza.

I felt as if I'd been disloyal or something.

Ridiculous, I told myself. Maritza was here, Mallory was back home.

Besides, if Mal came to visit, I'd have a chance to tell her everything.

If her parents let her visit.

If not, well, I'd tell her when I returned home.

But at the moment, I didn't want to think about that.

CHAPTER 11

"She's not in the departures waiting room!" shouted Maritza.

"Maybe she went outside by mistake," suggested Celeste.

"Where's the luggage claim?" asked Randy.

Maritza rolled her eyes. "This isn't the airport, it's Amtrak. People don't check luggage."

"Should we look for the lost and found?" Michael said.

"I think the police might be a better idea," Marian added.

What a mess.

Yes, Mallory's parents had agreed to let her visit. And I'd dragged my cousins and my friends to Penn Station to meet the train.

We'd arrived in time. We'd been there when the train pulled in. We'd watched the passengers emerge.

But no Mallory.

The Amtrak concourse is huge. But it's only part of Penn Station. Which means it's connected to the Long Island Railroad and Madison Square Garden in a maze of vaulted rooms, corridors, and tracks — on three different levels.

Mallory could be anywhere.

"Okay, don't panic," Michael said.

I wasn't panicking. Yet. I scanned the Amtrak concourse, trying to figure out where I'd be if I were her.

"Bagels," I said.

"This is no time for a snack!" Quint snapped.

"No. Mal loves bagels. If she got here and didn't see us, she may have gone into the bagel shop. I'll check there with Maritza. Michael, you check outside. Marian, you and Celeste look in the LIRR waiting room. Randy and Quint, you go back to the track, in case she was stuck in the train for some reason. Meet back here in ten minutes."

"Okay."

"Gotcha."

"Right."

We split up. As we raced through the crowd, I spotted a flash of reddish hair to my right.

"Jessi!"

Mallory was struggling toward me, holding a huge suitcase. "I'm sorry, I —"

"Mal!" I ran to her and threw my arms

around her. "I almost had a heart attack looking for you!"

"Well, I was at the back of the train. I must have come up the wrong stairway —"

"Maritza, this is Mallory. Mallory, Maritza." I took Mal's hand. "Come on, we have to meet the others."

One advantage of being a dancer: You can hop through crowds really fast. Well, except when you're pulling along a nondancer friend.

Randy, Quint, Marian, and Celeste soon arrived at our meeting place.

"She appears!" Randy exclaimed.

"Ta-da!" Celeste sang.

"Heyyyy, Mal!" Quint exclaimed, hugging her enthusiastically.

Mallory nearly fell over. "Uh, hi."

"Down, Rover," cracked Randy.

"You'll get used to them, Mal," Tanisha said. "They're dancers. They can't help being loud and physical."

Now Michael was walking toward us with a policeman.

"We found her!" I yelled.

As Michael shrugged at the policeman, Mallory turned beet red. "I'm sorry. I just came up the wrong —"

Everyone began talking at once — introducing themselves, asking questions, and just jab-bering away.

Michael let out a loud whistle. "I think we can find a better place to talk. Dinner at our apartment?"

"YEEEEAAAAA!"

Honestly, the people in Penn Station must have thought we were off the wall.

We surrounded Mallory, talking nonstop. Laughing like hyenas. Telling our funniest classroom stories.

I don't think she got a word in edgewise all the way to Michael and Marian's apartment.

As soon as we stepped inside, Michael took our dinner orders. Everyone wanted some-thing different — pizza, burgers, chicken, spaghetti.

"He's going to make all that?" Mallory asked.

We cracked up. "In New York, restaurants deliver," I explained. "Not just pizza. Anything you want."

Taking Mal's suitcase, I led her upstairs to my room.

Of course, the rest of my friends followed. As I set the suitcase down, they sat on the floor and the beds.

"Feels like a BSC meeting," Mallory said with a smile.

"A what?" Celeste asked.

"It's this club Mal and I belong to," I said.

Mallory looked surprised. "You haven't told them?"

I hadn't. The BSC, frankly, had been pretty far from my mind lately.

"I guess I meant to," I replied. "But —"

"Ooh!" Quint blurted out. "You will never, *ever* believe who I saw walking down Broadway after lunch! Mark Morris."

"No!" Maritza said. "Seriously?"

"Seriously," Quint replied. "I nodded hello and nearly ran into a fire hydrant. And he gives me this look, like, 'Yeah, right, who is this chump?'"

"That is almost as cool as the time I talked to Robert LaFosse in front of Lincoln Center," Maritza said.

I love these kinds of conversations. People have them all the time in New York. I call them Close Encounters of the Dance World.

Mallory wasn't saying much. At one point she leaned over to me and whispered, "Who are Mark Morris and Robert LaFosse?"

I couldn't believe it. To a ballet dancer, that's like asking who Steven Spielberg and Tom Cruise are. "A famous choreographer and dancer," I explained.

Mal nodded and listened patiently as we gossiped on.

Finally, Quint said to her, "We have such big

mouths. Tell us about you, Mal. Are you a ballet dancer? What level are you?"

Mal shook her head. "I don't dance."

"What do you like to do?" Maritza asked.

"Write stories," Mal replied. "Horse stories, especially. I love horses. And also I draw. Pictures."

"Uh-huh," said Maritza.

"Cool," said Quint.

Thunk, went an invisible blanket over the conversation.

Nod, nod, nod.

For the first time all day, the group was at a loss for words.

"Let's watch that video we made at Maritza's house," I suggested.

Zoom. Back downstairs.

We came to life again. We watched. We laughed. We talked. We ate.

Afterward, Marian and Michael took us all out to an ice-cream shop. Quint and Maritza entertained us with imitations of Toni and Mr. Brailsford. I demonstrated some of the choreography we were learning for our exhibition performance (and I nearly barfed up my mint chocolate chip hot fudge banana split).

The night went by so fast. By the time Mallory and I collapsed into our beds, it was after eleven o'clock.

"Tomorrow you'll meet Maritza's friends," I said.

Mallory laughed. "I thought I just did."

"No, her *neighborhood* friends," I explained. "The ones you saw in the video. So, how do you like my classmates? And New York? And my cousins? And how was your trip? You never even told me! And how's everybody back home?"

"Slow down!" Mallory said with a laugh. She was rummaging around in her suitcase now. "Oh, great. Jessi, I can't meet anybody tomorrow. I forgot a toothbrush. My breath'll scare away the pigeons."

"Not to worry." I ran to the top of the stairs. "Michael? Do you have an extra toothbrush for Mallory?"

"Nope," Michael called back up. "But I'll run down to the corner and get one."

"Thanks!" I said.

"A toothbrush *now*?" Mallory said. "It's almost midnight!"

"The greengrocer down the block is open twenty-four hours," I explained. "They sell everything there."

"Wow. All the shops in Stoneybrook close at nine."

"Hey. New York's the city that never sleeps."

"It kind of gets under your skin, doesn't it?

All that energy changes you. I can feel it."

"Yeah. I feel like a totally different person."

Mal nodded. "You've become so . . . I don't know, *forceful*. I mean, I sensed it the minute I saw you at the train station. The way you organized everyone to find me. Even the way you're talking — it's so *fast*."

"ReallyIdon'tknowwhatyoumean!" I said.

Mallory laughed. "Boy, I've missed you so much."

I wanted to say the same thing. But I couldn't. I was happy to see Mal, but I hadn't really *missed* her. I hadn't had time to. And I felt awful about that. So instead I just said, "Sorry I never call, Mal. I mean to. But I've just been so busy — school, homework, personal stuff."

"That's okay."

"I haven't even begun to tell you the details about Quint and me."

"Really?" Mallory sat on the bed and leaned forward eagerly. "I'm all ears."

Well, all I can say is, thank goodness it was Friday night.

By the time Mallory and I finished talking, it was almost two-thirty in the morning.

The first thing I did when I got up was call home.

Daddy pretended he'd forgotten my name.

He teased me about not being in touch. Mama listened intently as I told her my latest adventures. Aunt Cecelia reminded me to zip my coat and not wear my socks two days in a row. Becca basically grunted at me.

"She just misses you," Mallory explained. "When you're home again, she'll come around."

Michael and Marian came into the kitchen, showered and dressed. "Who wants omelettes?" Michael cried.

This time we did not order out. We *went* out, to the neighborhood coffee shop.

The weekend was off and running.

We hung out at Maritza's. Went to a movie. A performance of the American Ballet Theater. Dessert and jazz in Greenwich Village. A trip on the Staten Island ferry. The Empire State Building (about my seventh time). Lunch at Sylvia's in Harlem.

Before we knew it, Sunday afternoon had arrived and we were in a taxi, racing to Penn Station.

"I can't believe it's over," Mallory said.

"Wish you could stay longer," Michael said.

"Don't worry," I said. "I'm going to live here someday. Mal can be my roommate."

Mallory smiled. "I don't think I could ever live here. I mean, I love it, but it's too crazy."

"That's what I like about it," I said.

103

The taxi screeched to the curb. "Penn Station!" the cabdriver barked.

Marian quickly paid him. We scrambled out of the cab and ran into the station. Mallory's train was on the track, waiting to go. We barely had time for a hug before the doors closed.

Mallory was teary-eyed as she waved to us from the window. She kept mouthing "Thanks" and blowing us kisses.

"You have loyal friends," Marian said.

"What's she crying about?" Michael asked. "She's going to see Jessi in three days!"

Marian nudged him. "Listen to macho man over here."

I smiled. To tell the truth, though, I felt a little sad too.

But not for the same reason as Mal.

I was thinking about my own train trip home.

Back to Stoneybrook.

Back to baby-sitting and Mme Noelle. Early bedtimes and stores that close at nine at night. The downtown strip mall. Train stations too small to get lost in. The same old restaurants and movie theaters.

I had only three days until then.

Three days with my NYC friends. Three days of riding the subway like an old pro. Staying out late. Seeing the best ballet and theater on earth.

Not having to explain who Robert LaFosse is and what a *an de jamb* looks like.

I realized something awful.

In a way, I was relieved to see Mal leave.

More than that, though, I did not want to go home.

Ever.

CHAPTER 12

*T*hwonk! *Thud thud thud — crrrrrrunch! Boom boom boom boom — crrrrack!*

Have you ever been under a stage during a ballet? You would not believe the sound. No matter how delicate and graceful the choreography, you'd think hippos were fighting a war above you.

Our final-day performance was held in a small theater on the Lower East Side. As the B-Levels danced above us, we A-Levels waited in the dressing room/warm-up area below the stage.

I was warming up at the *barre*, between Maritza and Quint. "Ask your parents," Maritza said.

"I can't," I replied. "They're sitting upstairs."

"I mean, ask them after the show. It's only three more weeks. I'm staying for the extra session and so are Quint and Marcus and Celeste and Randy and Michiko."

"The tutors will still be here," Quint said. "You'll get school credit. I mean, if that's what your parents are worried about."

"Okay, I'll ask them," I said. "But I don't think they'll change their minds."

I was lying.

The truth?

Just about every A-Level student had been asked to stay for another three weeks. But I was one of the students who hadn't been.

I didn't know why. I didn't dare ask.

The worst thing was, Maritza and Quint had assumed that I'd been asked. And I'd been too chicken to admit the truth.

I could not think about that now. I had to shut out the disappointment. This was my last gasp as a Dance New York student.

"Okay, A-Level — places!" Toni yelled into the room. "Knock 'em dead!"

We all scampered upstairs. There we waited backstage while the B-Level students finished their ballet. As they took a curtain call, I peeked out into the audience.

I saw Mama, Daddy, Michael, Marian, and Aunt Cecelia. They'd all taken off from work to be at the show (except Aunt Cecelia, who doesn't have a job). They'd left Becca and Squirt with the Pikes, then raced to NYC.

Now they were in the first row. Inches from the stage.

"They're too close," I said.

"So?" Maritza asked.

"They *know* they're not supposed to sit close. You don't see choreography there. You see all the sweat and hear all the grunting and —"

"Chill, Jessi!" Quint said with a laugh.

"You're just working yourself up," Maritza added.

Easy for them to say. They had three more weeks. After this performance, I was out of here. Gone forever.

The crowd was quieting now. Mr. Brailsford was entering from the opposite side of the stage.

I felt Maritza grasping my hand. I looked at her. We let out tiny squeals and hugged each other.

"I said, *places!*" Toni insisted in a loud whisper.

We quickly formed a line.

I was shivering. I tried to swallow but I couldn't. My throat felt like a sandbox.

"Ladies and gentlemen," Mr. Brailsford was saying, "our youngest geniuses, and the future of ballet!"

Clang! went the opening chord on the piano.

Thump! went the lightboard as the lights flooded the stage.

Pow-pow-pow-pow went my heart.

"It's magic time," said Quint.

"Go!" hissed Toni.

My mind was all locked up. If I'd actually had to think, I would have been dead meat.

For three and a half weeks, Mr. Brailsford had been telling us, "Let your body think for you." For three and a half weeks, I'd been trying to figure out what that meant.

Now I knew.

My legs took over. They leaped and jumped from position to position.

Smile.

About two seconds into the dance, my face muscles chipped in. I may have been petrified inside, but outside I was beaming.

I was aware of the stage and the audience, but they were like a dream. All that mattered was the music, the steps, and my classmates. We were in a world of our own. A world that others could see but not enter.

I barely remember the performance. Well, except for one thing.

It happened toward the end of the dance, when Maritza and I cross the stage. Usually, in class, we make a face at each other. We try to crack each other up. It's like our own private contest.

This time, of course, we kept straight faces.

In that moment, I felt my world spinning away. I knew I'd never do this again. The faces, the jokes, the fun times — in just a few measures, they'd be over.

Push it aside.

Somehow I buried the feelings. I danced my heart out. As we hit the final tableau, I was practically hyperventilating.

Daddy shouted "Bravo!" before the rest of the audience started to applaud. His voice shocked me back into reality.

I could see him standing. He was pulling Aunt Cecelia to her feet. Mama was rising too.

All three of them had tears in their eyes.

That did it.

The floodgates opened.

All my emotions, everything that had been bottled up, spilled out.

Maritza's face was drenched in tears too. I grabbed her hand for our curtain call. It felt like a clammy wet rag.

"Sorry," she whimpered.

We burst out laughing. On top of the crying.

We could not stop. We must have looked so weird, crying and laughing at the same time as we curtsied to the audience.

We had to take two more curtain calls. Then Mr. Brailsford appeared stage right and handed each of us a flower. He told the audience, "Thank you for coming, and remember to keep your programs. Someday you'll be seeing these dancers again."

That, I will never forget.

Backstage, chaos broke loose. We couldn't

stop hugging each other. Every one of us was drenched in sweat, but no one cared.

"I will miss you so much, Jessi!" Celeste said.

"Write, okay?" Randy asked.

"You have our phone numbers," Michiko reminded me.

"Use E-mail," Marcus suggested.

"If you don't, I will personally come out to Donnybrook and bop you upside the head," Maritza vowed.

"Stoneybrook," I corrected her.

"Whatever."

That made us both howl again. And sob. We held each other tight, our shoulders heaving.

"I will never understand girls," Quint murmured.

The truth? His cheeks were a little moist too.

By that time, I wasn't even trying to dry my tears. Especially when my family came backstage. Mama and Daddy looked so proud.

I was in the middle of a big family hugfest when Mr. Brailsford approached us.

After I introduced him to everyone, he asked, "Where does she get her talent from?"

Daddy bellowed a laugh. "Not me! My wife lost two toes during our first dance."

"Well," Aunt Cecelia said, "I must say I'm not unfamiliar with the stage myself. You see, years ago —"

"Actually," Mr. Brailsford interrupted, "I

wondered if I might talk to you and your family, Jessi. Privately."

Oh, great. What now? He was going to explain why I hadn't been asked back. He wanted to recommend I try some other creative activity. Tap dancing, maybe. Or the trombone.

Why couldn't he just leave well enough alone?

"Sure," my dad said.

As we followed Mr. Brailsford toward a nearby exit, I glanced over my shoulder. Quint and Maritza were giving me curious looks.

I turned away. Mr. Brailsford was holding the door for us.

I took a deep breath and tried to smile.

But it was impossible.

I felt like a wet sponge. An invisible hand was squeezing me hard.

My joy was flowing out. I could almost see it disappearing between the floorboards.

CHAPTER 13

Wednesday

Mal and I baby-sat for the Pike tribe today. They were fine. Nothing unusual or bad or interesting happened.

For the record, Becca and Squirt were there too. Becca went home with Vanessa after school, and the Ramseys had dropped Squirt off around lunchtime on their way to the Big Apple. The City That Never Sleeps! The Dance Capital of the World !!

Ahem. Mallory, please. Stick to the topic. The sitting job.

Sorry, Kristy. Okay, well, later after Mom returned from running errands, and Dad came home from work we all had to rush to the BSC meeting, so we brought Becca with us.

And now a comment from one of our special guests.

BECCA WAS HEAR !!!!!!!!! !! ! !!! ! !!

That entry was written during the Wednesday BSC meeting. As you can tell, everyone was a little excited.

They were not, however, telling the whole story.

The BSC had big, secret plans for that evening.

It all started during the sitting job. Mallory was playing her parents' cassette tape of the musical *On the Town*, which is about New York.

She was singing along too. Using a brass candleholder as a microphone.

Mallory may not be much of a dancer, but she's an even worse singer. Her brothers and sisters were practically on the floor laughing.

Not Squirt and Becca. They must have showbiz blood, like me. Squirt was bouncing along, squealing at the top of his lungs. And shy Becca was singing with the tape in an operatic voice. Well, sort of.

"You Nork, You No-o-ork!" she hooted.

"What's a nork?" Claire asked.

"The Bronx is up and the Battery's down," Mallory warbled. "And Jessi's coming home tonight. . . ."

Vanessa groaned. "That doesn't rhyme!"

"What's a nork?" Claire repeated.

"You are," Nicky replied. "A total nork."

"Silly-billy-goo-goo," Claire said, storming toward the kitchen.

Rrrrrinnng! went the kitchen phone.

"Hello, Claire speaking," Claire's voice piped up.

"We never rhy-y-y-yme!" Becca sang to the final chords of the song. "And it's party ti-i-i-ime!"

"Bravo!" Margo yelled.

"Boo!" said Adam. "Boring!"

Normally, Mallory would have scolded Adam. But she was busy hatching an idea. "Becca, do your parents have plans for tonight? Like, dinner out or something?"

Becca shook her head. "Just picking up Squirt and me at seven. Then we're going home."

"Not if we force them to stay," Mal said, "for a surprise party. I mean, if —"

"YEEEEEEAAAAAH!" screamed the Pike kids.

"Can we invite Charlotte?" asked Becca. "And Natalie Springer and Haley Braddock?"

"*If* Mom and Dad let us have the party," Mal continued.

"Isn't this kind of short notice?" Stacey asked.

"Yeah. But it can't hurt to ask. We'll get Kristy to help us. We can invite the rest of the BSC, and we'll go shopping after our meeting."

"I want to go shopping too!" Becca insisted. "And to the meeting."

"Meemee!" Squirt echoed.

"I just hope your parents are in a fabulous mood," Stacey remarked.

Well, they were. They agreed to Mal's idea, but only after Mal insisted the BSC would do all the work.

Stacey and Mal ran off to the meeting, taking Becca with them.

When they mentioned their plan, Kristy declared Emergency Surprise Party Mobilization. "Man the phones!" she cried.

"*Person* the phones," Abby corrected her.

One by one, everyone phoned home for permission to go to the party. Becca called her friends too. Between those calls and our clients, the receiver was off the hook the entire half hour.

Becca was fascinated. By the end of the meeting, she was begging to join the BSC. (I'm sure she was an absolute pain, but no one complained to me.)

Claudia's parents agreed to chauffeur several BSC members to the store. (Mr. Pike took the rest in one of the Pikes' station wagons.)

An hour later, the Pike house was full of busy kids.

Vanessa, Margo, and Nicky made a huge WELCOME HOME, JESSI banner. Mallory used the family computer to print out a ballerina icon, with the words A STAR RETURNS printed underneath.

Becca, Haley, and Natalie "helped" Mr. Pike make chocolate chip cookies. Next to them, the triplets were supposedly making fruit punch. (Mr. Pike made two batches of cookies, but one *disappeared* almost immediately.)

Mrs. Pike ordered pizzas by phone. The others busied themselves with salad making and cleanup.

By 7:00 the surprise was ready. The living room was decorated. The pizzas were keeping warm in the oven. The cookies (or what was left of them) were sitting on a platter under plastic wrap.

At 7:06 Mallory heard an approaching car. "She's coming! Turn off the lights."

Mr. and Mrs. Pike stood by the front door. The others found hiding places out of sight of the front window.

The car puttered by.

"False alarm," Mr. Pike said.

"Rats," Margo muttered.

Claire stood up and walked toward the kitchen. "I'm hungry!"

"Get back," whispered Jordan. "You'll spoil the surprise."

"No fair," Claire murmured, shuffling back to her hiding place.

Everyone remained silent for about two minutes.

Then Byron cried out, "Aaauuuggggh!" and tumbled to the living room floor.

"Sssshhh!" hissed Adam.

"Nicky farted!" Byron howled.

"Did not!" Nicky protested.

"*Guys*, cut it out," Mr. Pike said.

Two more minutes of silence.

Vanessa started snoring. That made everyone crack up.

Then came a round of burping.

Animal noises.

Bird calls.

At 7:20, Kristy asked, "Do you think they went home first?"

Mallory called my number, but the machine was on.

"They must have hit traffic," Mrs. Pike said.

Claire giggled. "That's silly. Why would they hit cars?"

By 7:25, everyone was sitting on the sofa, eating chips and pretzels.

At 7:35 Mr. Pike brought out the pizzas. "Might as well eat them before they harden. We can always get more when Jessi comes."

At 7:45, Mrs. Pike tried our number again and left another message.

At eight o'clock, Charlotte, Haley, and Natalie had to go home. Mary Anne left with them, and walked them to their parents' cars on the way. "Call me when they show up," she said.

Mallory paced the living room. The triplets and Abby were playing Monopoly while Claire played Sorry with Kristy, Stacey, and Claudia. Vanessa was scribbling in a notebook. Margo and Nicky were in the den, watching TV. Mr. and Mrs. Pike were reading the newspaper.

"I'm surprised they haven't called," Kristy remarked.

"They did," Claire said.

Adam rolled his eyes. "Uh, Claire, do you know what *fantasy* means?"

"They *did*!" Claire insisted. "I talked to them."

Mallory's ears pricked up. "You mean, when the phone rang before while we were singing, and you picked up? That was *them*?"

"Yup," Claire replied proudly.

Now everyone was looking at her.

"What did they say?" Mrs. Pike asked.

"That they were coming."

"Coming *when*?" Mallory asked.

"Late," Claire replied.

"They said they were going to be late, and you didn't tell us?" Byron said, practically yelling.

Claire made a face at him. "We already knew that! *Everyone* knows nighttime is late!"

Jordan and Adam groaned out loud.

The rest of them kept it in. But barely.

When did my parents show up? At 9:10.

By that time, Kristy and Abby had left. The lights were blazing in the house. The cookies and pizza were gone. But everyone yelled "Surprise!" anyway.

"Where were you?" Becca asked.

"Didn't you get the message?" Daddy said.

"I instructed Claire to tell you we were to be late," Aunt Cecelia said.

"See?" Claire said proudly.

Mallory was looking around them, toward the empty porch. "Where's Jessi?"

Mama and Daddy looked at each other. "Well, uh, something came up," Mama said. "An audition. She has to stay in New York. But just one more night."

"She'll be here tomorrow afternoon," Daddy added.

"Oh," Mallory replied. "I guess the surprise was on us."

She was not happy.

Not at all.

CHAPTER 14

At five o'clock on Thursday morning, I was wide-awake.

I'd been dreaming about the previous afternoon. The images were running through my mind, over and over again.

Stepping out into the hallway after the performance. Feeling about two inches tall. Wanting to run away.

And then Mr. Brailsford turning to my parents and saying, "Mr. and Mrs. Ramsey, I'm about to ask you something I very rarely ask of parents."

Very rarely. That was how he put it.

I was a basket case.

"I'd like Jessica to audition for the Dance New York education program, full-time."

The words didn't compute at first. As if Mr. Brailsford had suddenly switched to Lithuanian.

"Audition?" Aunt Cecelia spoke up. "But you already know how she dances."

"You're right," Mr. Brailsford said. "However, all decisions about full-time students are made by a committee, including the other teachers. And they need to see Jessica. If they like her as much as I do, she's in."

It was sinking in. I was light-headed. He was singling me out.

My future was racing before my eyes. My name in lights.

I wanted to scream. I bit my lip.

"Well," Daddy said. "Well. That's an honor."

"You mean, she would have to leave home?" Mama said. "Live in New York City?"

"Is this a boarding school?" Aunt Cecelia asked.

Mr. Brailsford shook his head. "Sometimes students stay with relatives. Or a parent takes an apartment in the city. If neither of these is an option, we can help place students with the families of classmates."

Mama's brow was all furrowed. "I have to admit, I feel funny about this."

"Let's not jump the gun," Michael spoke up. "He's asking Jessi to *audition*. She has to earn the spot first."

"Of course she'll earn the spot, Michael!" Aunt Cecelia snapped. "Must you be so negative?"

"You needn't make a decision right now," Mr. Brailsford said. "We can squeeze in the audition tomorrow before the start of classes. Then, if Jessica makes it, she can start at any time — now, next semester, next year . . ."

"The important question is," Daddy said, looking me squarely in the eye, "is this what *you* want, Jessi?"

The word "yes" left my mouth before I could put a thought together.

"Michael and I would be happy to have Jessi another night," Marian said.

Mama and Daddy exchanged a long look. Then Mama nodded.

"Well," Daddy said with a sigh, "I suppose the audition is the easy part of the decision. We'll worry about the hard part later, if we need to. Your mama and I think you should at least have the opportunity. I'll contact SMS and let your teachers know you'll be absent. I can leave work early tomorrow and drive in to pick you up at five-thirty."

"Really?" was the only word I could manage to say.

"I'm delighted," Mr. Brailsford said. "See you at the studio tomorrow morning, fifteen minutes before the session? We'll make sure Jessi has plenty of activity the rest of the day. She'll be with the kids who are starting the new session."

I don't know how I kept my cool as we said our good-byes.

The moment we stepped onto the elevator, I nearly exploded with joy. I wrapped my arms around Mama and Daddy and thanked them a million times. I didn't care who was watching us.

"I say we head to Chinatown for a family celebration!" Daddy declared.

Outside on the sidewalk, Maritza, Tanisha, and Quint were waiting. When I told them what happened, they shrieked.

"What if you make it?" Maritza asked. "Will you accept?"

"I guess I'll have to work it out," I replied.

"You'll never regret it," Tanisha added. "I haven't."

"If you have any doubts, call me," Quint said. "It's payback time. I owe you for Juilliard."

Aunt Cecelia was nodding proudly. "They're right, Jessi. *They're* not wasting their talents."

I could see Michael rolling his eyes. "Unlike me, huh?" he muttered under his breath.

"John, what about Becca and Squirt?" Mama was asking Daddy.

"While I get the car, would someone call the Pikes and tell them we'll be late?" Daddy asked.

Aunt Cecelia agreed. She walked off to a pay phone while Daddy jogged to the car lot.

How was Chinatown? Fun, but I was already

nervous about my audition. I could hardly eat.

Anyway, I was thinking about all of that on Thursday morning, as I lay in bed. And my stomach was beginning to grumble.

I tried to go back to sleep. No way. So I got dressed and went to the kitchen to fix myself breakfast.

Marian and Michael must have heard me. They emerged soon after. Michael made us oatmeal, while Marian put on a soothing jazz CD. That helped calm my nerves.

I was silent as I rode the subway into Manhattan with Michael.

I tried to look cheerful as I walked into the studio.

Behind a table sat five grim, tired faces. The other Dance New York instructors. I'd seen them in the hallways but never met them.

As Mr. Brailsford introduced me, I could feel my knees starting to knock.

Fortunately, Toni entered the room then. She has such a warm smile. I immediately felt at ease.

"Let's start," Mr. Brailsford said, walking toward me. "If something's not clear, just stop me."

My mouth nearly hit the floor.

He — Mr. Brailsford himself — was going to give me the combination.

Talk about difficult. This combination was impossible.

He went through each step about three times. I tried to follow. I tried to memorize. I practiced several times alone, with the piano accompaniment.

"Okay, let's see what you've got," barked one of the teachers.

I died. I blew it. Egg on face.

"Let me try again!" I pleaded.

"It's early," Toni said with a smile. "I can barely walk at this hour."

Right.

I took a deep breath. I thought to myself, *Where there's a will, there's a way.*

And I tried again.

This time I made it through. The instructors were all scribbling away, whispering among themselves.

Mr. Brailsford quickly taught me a second, jazzier piece.

I was feeling confident now. I performed that one too. I even added a flourish of my own at the end.

The fifteen minutes seemed to pass in a few seconds. The teachers smiled and left for class.

I felt totally wrung out.

"Very nice, Jessica," Mr. Brailsford said as I wiped my face with a towel.

"If you want to call me back or something," I said, "I'll be in Stoneybrook tonight —"

Mr. Brailsford shook his head. "I won't be calling you back. We've seen enough."

Ugh. My breath caught in my throat. I felt as if he'd punched me in the stomach.

"That's okay," I said, fighting back tears. "I really enjoyed it, and —"

"There's no pressure, of course," Mr. Brailsford said. "You can choose to start right away or wait for the spring session. Even next fall, if your parents prefer —"

"Start? You mean — ?"

Mr. Brailsford smiled warmly. "Jessica, I knew from the beginning. I just had to let my colleagues see you. They agree with me. You're in. You're one of us now."

CHAPTER 15

"And then he said —" I dropped my voice as deeply as I could. " 'You're one of us now.' "

"He didn't!" Mama exclaimed.

"He sure did," Daddy said.

Aunt Cecelia raised her eyebrows. "*You* weren't there."

"No, but I heard the story several times on the way home," Daddy replied.

"He sounds like Darth Vader," Becca remarked.

"So I can start tomorrow if I want," I said. "I already met some of the kids in the full-time program. They're really nice and —"

"Jessicaaaaa," Daddy said in his warning voice. "We talked about this in the car. You know this is going to take some hard thinking."

"So let's think now," I said. "I mean, I called Michael and Marian after the audition. They said I can stay with them."

"I know, darling," Mama said. "Michael called us too."

Aunt Cecelia was smiling. "He's grateful to you, Jessi. You inspired him, you know. He's started painting again. He told me he really wants your dream to come true."

I could hear pride in Aunt Cecelia's voice. That made me feel good. She ought to appreciate her son.

"I feel it would be too much to ask of them," Daddy said. "They're a busy young couple. As much as they love you, we can't ask them to be your guardians year-round."

"I wish one of us could take an apartment in the city," Mama said. "But that would mean quitting a job and losing that income *plus* paying the rent on the apartment. Besides, it wouldn't be fair to Becca and Squirt."

"Yeah," Becca said.

"I could commute," I suggested.

"That's over four hours of traveling every day," said Daddy.

Mama looked horrified. "Alone?"

"I'd meet her at the Stoneybrook station," Aunt Cecelia said.

"Fine, but what about in New York?" Daddy asked. "How would she get to Grand Central Station at the end of the day?"

"You might get mugged," Becca piped up.

"I could ask one of the other kids to take the subway with me," I said.

"Two eleven-year-olds riding the subway alone?" Mama said.

"I'm not a baby!" I exclaimed.

"She's right," Aunt Cecelia agreed.

Daddy glared at her.

Mama sighed. "Look, Jessi, it's late. We're all tired. I don't want to argue and wake up your brother. Let's sleep on this. It's a complicated issue. And the transportation is only part of it. Even if by some miracle we worked it out, you still have a lot to think about. Do you really want to leave Stoneybrook — your school, your friends, the Baby-sitters Club?"

I didn't have an answer to that one.

In fact, the question kept me up most of the night.

Could I give everything up?

I loved my New York friends. I'd had the best time with them. I hadn't even missed the BSC that much.

But now that I was home, I couldn't wait to talk to Mal. Or my other BSC friends.

I thought about our school trip to Hawaii. About a bus ride we took through this gorgeous mountain scenery on the island of Oahu. I had vowed to myself I would someday move to Hawaii. But I couldn't help noticing that a few people on the bus were fast asleep. "Commuters," Stacey had said. "They probably see this every day."

I remember thinking: If you can be bored with this, you can be bored with anything. Better to be a visitor. That way, scenery will always be spectacular and romantic.

Well, I had been a visitor to New York. And it was spectacular and romantic too.

What would happen if I moved there? Would it become routine, the way Hawaii had become for those commuters? Would I be caught up in the competition and professionalism, like Tanisha? Always worrying about auditions and injuries?

Would that be worth leaving Stoneybrook, my family, and my friends for?

I drifted off. I never did find the answer.

Boy, did it feel good to see Claudia, Stacey, Mal, and Mary Anne the next morning. They were waiting for me on the corner of Locust and Fawcett — the way it's been every morning before school. As if I'd never left.

"Welcome back!" Stacey shouted, throwing her arms around me.

"Are you a star yet?" Claudia asked.

"She is around here," Mary Anne said.

They were full of questions. I had time to tell them only a fraction of what had happened.

They told me about the so-called surprise party, but just briefly. Claudia quickly changed the subject. "So, how did your audition go?"

"Fine," I said.

"Are you going to be in some big ballet or something?" Claudia asked.

"Unfortunately, no." It was my turn to change the subject. "So, tell me everything that happened here."

Okay, I didn't mention a thing about Mr. Brailsford's offer.

I didn't want to.

For something this big, I wanted to talk to Mal alone first.

I planned to bring it up at our lockers. But I chickened out.

At lunch, I managed to tell her about my final week. Well, most of it. A few other friends sat at our table, and I had to repeat my story from the beginning a few times.

It wasn't until later, on our walk home, that we had some privacy.

That was when Mallory told me the full story of the surprise party. She tried hard to make it sound funny. Like something out of a sitcom.

But it wasn't funny.

And I felt guilty.

"I can't believe no one at home told me about this," I said.

"Becca probably forgot," Mallory said with a

laugh. "And I guess your mom and dad didn't want you to feel bad."

"Well, I do. You all showed up, and I finked out."

"It wasn't your fault. We just shouldn't let Claire take messages."

I pictured the room full of people. My friends. All waiting for me. All pulling together at a moment's notice.

Would my friendships with Maritza and Quint and Tanisha and Celeste be as close?

Could any friendships ever be as close?

Maybe.

Maybe not.

"So, what was your audition for?" Mallory asked.

Gulp. Sweating time.

"For a different ballet program," I replied.

"Really? How did you do?"

"Pretty well."

"Great."

I braced myself for the questions: *What program?* and *Are you going away again?*

But Mallory never asked.

So I didn't say another word about it.

I wasn't ready to.

I'd been wrong. I didn't need to talk to Mallory about my decision.

I needed to make it myself.

We said good-bye and I headed home.

My mind was going a mile a minute as I walked in my front door. I could hear Becca inside playing with Squirt. Aunt Cecelia was sitting on the living room sofa, reading a newspaper.

"Welcome home, darling," she said.

I sat next to her. "Aunt Cecelia, you really do want me to become a ballerina, don't you?"

Aunt Cecelia put down her paper. "Jessica Ramsey, are you trying to get me to convince your parents to send you away?"

"No! I just want an honest answer."

"Well, if you must know, yes, I do. Nothing would make me happier."

"So you think I should go?"

"Jessica, Jessica," Aunt Cecelia said with a sigh. "What can I say? I will never stand in the way of your future. But everything in its time, darling. And you have a lot of time on your hands. Think about that."

Aunt Cecelia's words stuck in my brain.

I thought about time. And timing.

I guess you have to, when you're making the biggest decision of your life.

Dance New York really had happened at the right time in my life. It had given me so much. It had made me feel happy and confident. It had made me realize I could live away from home. Be a leader.

Now I had the opportunity to go back. For

more of the same thing. Was this happening at the right time too?

Sure, I'd have to give up some things. My walks to school. The Baby-sitters Club. Seeing my little brother and sister every day. Evenings around the dinner table. Graduating from Stoneybrook Middle School with my best friends. Spending my teen years in my own house with my family. My best friend.

What would I gain? A better chance of being a professional dancer someday.

Maybe.

Tanisha had said most of the students don't make it. And everyone knows that ballet stars come from all over the country. They train in many different places. Places like the Stamford Ballet School.

This was so confusing. Images from the past month were tumbling around in my head.

I thought about Quint. About how he wanted so badly to be my boyfriend. How afraid I'd been! How scared that he'd hate me for telling him the truth.

But I'd stuck to my convictions. I'd had to. And Quint had understood. Nothing awful had happened. We're still friends. The timing just wasn't right for anything more.

Timing is important.

Very important.

"A penny for your thoughts," Aunt Cecelia said.

I took a deep breath.

"I've made up my mind," I declared.

I was surprised at my own words. But the jumble was beginning to clear.

"Oh?"

"I'm going to accept —"

"Oh, dear," Aunt Cecelia muttered. "I do not plan to be within a mile of this house when your father and mother arrive home."

"When I'm a little older," I continued.

Aunt Cecelia squinted at me. "Beg pardon?"

"It's timing, Aunt Cecelia. Right now, I belong here. With you and Becca and Squirt and Mama and Daddy —"

"Yes, of course you do, but —"

"Don't try to change my mind. I'm not going to give up dancing. Mr. Brailsford said the offer will stay open. So until then, I'll go to class and get better and better. And maybe someday . . ." I shrugged.

"Off to the big time," Aunt Cecelia said.

"Right."

"I like the way you think, Jessica." Aunt Cecelia smiled. "Now, if you would only give your cousin another little nudge about his artwork. . . ."

I gave Aunt Cecelia a big kiss on the cheek and ran to my room.

I didn't let her finish her sentence.

But she didn't mind.

I could tell.

Dear Reader,

In *Jessi's Big Break*, Jessi has the adventure of her ballet lifetime. Not only does she get to attend a prestigious ballet school but she gets to live in New York City with a group of new friends with whom she has a lot in common. Jessi finds she loves living in Brooklyn and that being a kid in New York is not as different from being a kid in Stoneybrook as she had thought it would be. She can visit her friends at their apartments. They can order pizza and have a party. She also finds that, unlike in Stoneybrook, she can order in any kind of food at any hour of the day. Plus, she can go to a movie — *or* she can go to a Broadway show, a jazz club, a museum, or an art gallery. Instead of being driven in a car when she wants to go somewhere, she can take the subway.

Being a kid in New York is exciting! Jessi loved every minute of her visit. You can see why she had a hard time deciding whether to leave Dance NY!

Happy reading,

Ann M Martin

Ann M. Martin

About the Author

ANN MATTHEWS MARTIN was born on August 12, 1955. She grew up in Princeton, NJ, with her parents and her younger sister, Jane.

Although Ann used to be a teacher and then an editor of children's books, she's now a full-time writer. She gets ideas for her books from many different places. Some are based on personal experiences. Others are based on childhood memories and feelings. Many are written about contemporary problems or events.

All of Ann's characters, even the members of the Baby-sitters Club, are made up. (So is Stoneybrook.) But many of her characters are based on real people. Sometimes Ann names her characters after people she knows, other times she chooses names she likes.

In addition to the Baby-sitters Club books, Ann Martin has written many other books for children. Her favorite is *Ten Kids, No Pets* because she loves big families and she loves animals. Her favorite Baby-sitters Club book is *Kristy's Big Day*. (By the way, Kristy is her favorite baby-sitter!)

Ann M. Martin now lives in New York with her cats, Gussie and Woody. Her hobbies are reading, sewing, and needlework — especially making clothes for children.

Notebook Pages

This Baby-sitters Club book belongs to _____.

I am _____ years old and in the _____

grade.

The name of my school is _____.

I got this BSC book from _____.

I started reading it on _____ and

finished reading it on _____.

The place where I read most of this book is _____.

My favorite part was when _____.

If I could change anything in the story, it might be the part when

_____.

My favorite character in the Baby-sitters Club is _____.

The BSC member I am most like is _____

because _____.

If I could write a Baby-sitters Club book it would be about _____

_____.

#115 Jessi's Big Break

In *Jessi's Big Break*, one of Jessi's biggest dreams comes true — she gets to dance with a world-famous dance company! My biggest dream is to _____

_____. The closest I came to this dream was when _____

_____. Jessi is thrilled to take lessons with David Brailsford, a famous dancer and choreographer. If I could take lessons with anyone, I would take them with _____

_____ because _____.

Jessi has to make a big choice when David Brailsford asks her to join Dance NY full-time. Jessi decides to stay at SMS (for the time being). If I were Jessi, I would have chosen to _____

_____ because _____

_____. If I had a chance to move to New York City, I would (or would not) want to go because _____

_____. If I could go to school anywhere in the world, I would pick _____

_____.

JESSI'S

This is me at age four.

Me with my new baby brother.

I'm always happy when I'm dancing.

SCRAPBOOK

Matt and Haley Braddock, two of my favorite charges.

My family— Daddy and Mama Becca, me, Aunt Cecelia and Squirt.

Read all the books
about **Jessi**
in the Baby-sitters Club series
by Ann M. Martin

Look for #116

ABBY AND THE BEST KID EVER

The water was mopped up almost as quickly as it had been spilled, but Lou kept apologizing. "It wasn't Happy's fault," she insisted. "But I didn't mean to do it. I'm really, really sorry."

"Chill, Lou," said Jay, giving her a grin and a punch on the arm. "Maybe we won't have to take baths tonight."

"And maybe you will," said Mrs. McNally, laughing.

Lou didn't laugh.

Mr. McNally said, "Well, I guess we've done all we can do today. Let's get back to the motel."

"Can we give you a ride home, Abby?" Mrs. McNally asked.

"That'd be great," I answered.

So the McNallys drove me home. As I got out of the car, Jay said, "See you later, alligator."

"In a while, crocodile," I answered.

Jay laughed as if I'd said the funniest thing ever, and Mr. and Mrs. McNally grinned.

But Lou only smiled a small smile and said, "Thank you, Abby."

"You're welcome, Lou," I answered. I waved as they drove away. I couldn't wait to tell the BSC the news. Lou McNally, the Worst Kid Ever, had somehow been magically transformed into the Princess of Perfect.

THE BABY-SITTERS CLUB®

Collect them all!

More titles... ➤

The Baby-sitters Club titles continued...

❏ MG22873-0	#89	Kristy and the Dirty Diapers	$3.50
❏ MG22874-9	#90	Welcome to the BSC, Abby	$3.99
❏ MG22875-1	#91	Claudia and the First Thanksgiving	$3.50
❏ MG22876-5	#92	Mallory's Christmas Wish	$3.50
❏ MG22877-3	#93	Mary Anne and the Memory Garden	$3.99
❏ MG22878-1	#94	Stacey McGill, Super Sitter	$3.99
❏ MG22879-X	#95	Kristy + Bart = ?	$3.99
❏ MG22880-3	#96	Abby's Lucky Thirteen	$3.99
❏ MG22881-1	#97	Claudia and the World's Cutest Baby	$3.99
❏ MG22882-X	#98	Dawn and Too Many Sitters	$3.99
❏ MG69205-4	#99	Stacey's Broken Heart	$3.99
❏ MG69206-2	#100	Kristy's Worst Idea	$3.99
❏ MG69207-0	#101	Claudia Kishi, Middle School Dropout	$3.99
❏ MG69208-9	#102	Mary Anne and the Little Princess	$3.99
❏ MG69209-7	#103	Happy Holidays, Jessi	$3.99
❏ MG69210-0	#104	Abby's Twin	$3.99
❏ MG69211-9	#105	Stacey the Math Whiz	$3.99
❏ MG69212-7	#106	Claudia, Queen of the Seventh Grade	$3.99
❏ MG69213-5	#107	Mind Your Own Business, Kristy!	$3.99
❏ MG69214-3	#108	Don't Give Up, Mallory	$3.99
❏ MG69215-1	#109	Mary Anne to the Rescue	$3.99
❏ MG05988-2	#110	Abby the Bad Sport	$3.99
❏ MG05989-0	#111	Stacey's Secret Friend	$3.99
❏ MG05990-4	#112	Kristy and the Sister War	$3.99
❏ MG45575-3		Logan's Story Special Edition Readers' Request	$3.25
❏ MG47118-X		Logan Bruno, Boy Baby-sitter Special Edition Readers' Request	$3.50
❏ MG47756-0		Shannon's Story Special Edition	$3.50
❏ MG47686-6		The Baby-sitters Club Guide to Baby-sitting	$3.25
❏ MG47314-X		The Baby-sitters Club Trivia and Puzzle Fun Book	$2.50
❏ MG48400-1		BSC Portrait Collection: Claudia's Book	$3.50
❏ MG22864-1		BSC Portrait Collection: Dawn's Book	$3.50
❏ MG69181-3		BSC Portrait Collection: Kristy's Book	$3.99
❏ MG22865-X		BSC Portrait Collection: Mary Anne's Book	$3.99
❏ MG48399-4		BSC Portrait Collection: Stacey's Book	$3.50
❏ MG69182-1		BSC Portrait Collection: Abby's Book	$3.99
❏ MG92713-2		The Complete Guide to The Baby-sitters Club	$4.95
❏ MG47151-1		The Baby-sitters Club Chain Letter	$14.95
❏ MG48295-5		The Baby-sitters Club Secret Santa	$14.95
❏ MG45074-3		The Baby-sitters Club Notebook	$2.50
❏ MG44783-1		The Baby-sitters Club Postcard Book	$4.95

Available wherever you buy books...or use this order form.

Scholastic Inc., P.O. Box 7502, Jefferson City, MO 65102

Please send me the books I have checked above. I am enclosing $_____
(please add $2.00 to cover shipping and handling). Send check or money order—
no cash or C.O.D.s please.

Name_____Birthdate_____

Address_____

City_____State/Zip_____

BSC5962

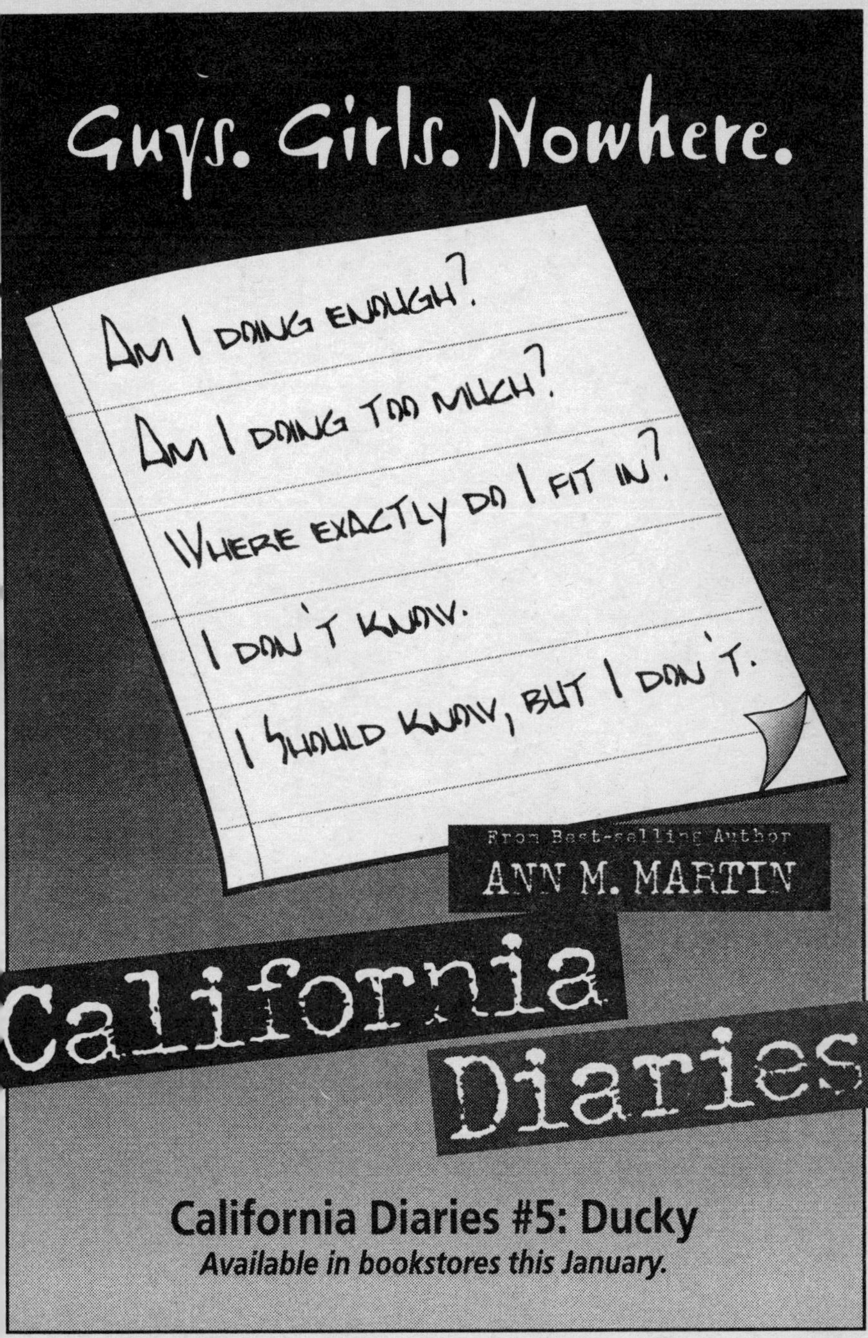
Guys. Girls. Nowhere.
Am I doing enough?
Am I doing too much?
Where exactly do I fit in?
I don't know.
I should know, but I don't.
From Best-selling Author
ANN M. MARTIN
California Diaries
California Diaries #5: Ducky
Available in bookstores this January.